I0600519

Beauty and the Beast. Really.

A Musical Comedy

Book, Music and Lyrics by
Rick Abbot

A SAMUEL FRENCH ACTING EDITION

SAMUEL
FRENCH
FOUNDED 1830
New York Hollywood London Toronto
SAMUELFRENCH.COM

Samuel French, Inc. can lend you a piano vocal score for a period of 8 weeks only upon receipt of the following:

1. Number of performances and exact performance dates.
2. Deposit of $25.00, which is refunded on the safe return of the score immediately after your production.
3. A musical rental fee of $10.00 *for each* performance planned.
4. $3.00 to cover postage and handling.

Please note that Samuel French, Inc. cannot fill any order for music unless it is accompanied by remittance above, as all rental material is handled on a strictly c.o.d. basis.

CAST OF CHARACTERS

BEAUTY — an absolutely stunning young lady
BEAST — an absolutely repulsive monster
LULA — Beauty's reasonably pretty stepsister
FATHER — a somewhat stolid farm-owner
HOLGA — Father's somewhat stolid wife
BEAU — a handsome young bucolic swain
HARRY — an ambitious theatrical entrepreneur
MAXINE — a not-very-talented tap dancer
SAM — a faithful and rather large hound dog

[Note: Total membership of the cast of this show is 3 males and 4 females, no matter what the foregoing list would lead you to believe otherwise.]

TIME: Days of Yore
PLACE: A small farm near an enchanted forest and a large castle within that forest

This play has two acts, during which the locale shifts constantly between the farm and the castle of the Beast

Any resemblance between the characters in this show and the characters in the original tale by the Brothers Grimm is to be considered a minor miracle.

4

MUSICAL NUMBERS

ACT ONE

OVERTURE........................Accompanist
"Someday Someone"/"That Girl!"......Beauty/Holga
"A Heart That's Happy" ....Beau, Lula
"Environmental Outlook" . Father, Holga, Beauty, Lula
"He Ought to Be Mine".......................Lula
"A Simple Little Rose".... Father, Holga, Beauty, Lula
"Somebody Is Hiding".................Beast, Father
"Whatta Ya Think o' That?"...........Beast, Father
"Tra-La!"..........................Beauty, Lula
"When the Children Are Gone".........Father, Holga

ACT TWO

ENTR'ACTE ....Accompanist
"This Must Be the Place" ....Beauty, Lula, Beast
"The Witch's Curse" ....Beast, Lula, Beauty
"Such a Time We Had!"..............Father, Holga
"Searching for Someone" ....Beast, Lula
"Someday Someone"/"That Girl!" ....Lula/Beauty
"Back on the Farm" ....Beauty, Lula
"The Beast Is Dead"......................Principals
"Isn't It Kinda Great?" ....Entire Cast

AND

MAXINE'S MUSIC [whenever least expected]. Accompanist

5

For
STEPHEN SONDHEIM,
the greatest composer in the
history of music, marvelous
mentor, and loyal friend

SPECIAL NOTE ON LIGHTING FOR THIS SHOW

There are two alternating sets, the farm and the castle. Despite all the references to darkness, gloom, etc., lighting for either place is always FULL BRIGHTNESS during *activity* in each area. When *no* activity — that is, *story-line* activity — is happening onstage, LIGHTING REDUCES TO ONE-THIRD NORMAL.

Because MAXINE appears frequently in this show, it would be tiresome to list the lighting-effects each time she does so, for director and author alike. Therefore, when the stage direction reads, *"MAXINE does her thing,"* here is what happens:

1) After first 6 notes (5 counts) of her INTRO MUSIC, on the next count — instantly — STAGE LIGHTS GO TO ONE-THIRD, and a FOLLOW-SPOT HITS MAXINE. Until spot hits her, MAXINE is rather slumped and weary, but as soon as spot hits, she flashes all 32 teeth, perks up to full peppiness, and does her dance. This dance consists in her tapping (exactly 8 taps to the bar) from stage left (where she *always* enters) to center stage, where she will dance with more wild enthusiasm than talent, leaving herself just enough melody to leave center stage, tap over to the sign-holding placard at extreme downstage right, and either *remove* the top card (which she only does the first time she dances) which says "BEAUTY AND THE BEAST. REALLY." in large garish lettering, and rather clumsily fling it offstage right, *or* flip the card over which is beneath the show-title card; this second card says "THE FARM" on one side, and "THE CASTLE" on the other. When she has flung or flipped, as the case may be, she always com-

pletes her dance in the same way: On final note, she will be body-facing offstage right, but head-facing audience; her right hand will be on nearest top corner of easel, her left hand on her waist, left elbow thrust backward; her head will toss back/left with her mouth partly open in an all-teeth-bared "starlet" smile; and her left knee will rise slightly, and left foot point backward toward stage left (her legs would — from audience point-of-view — be forming a numeral "4"); this *all* happens on final note. Then, exactly one beat later, the follow-spot goes out, and MAXINE — fully visible in that one-third lighting, but behaving as though she were no longer being seen — will sag, arms dangling at sides, head forward and down, and then shuffle off wearily into the stage right wings.

2) *During* MAXINE's number, in that one-third lighting upstage of her, cast members and crew members will be shifting from the farm-set to the castle-set, or vice-versa, as the script requires, *additionally lighted by a strobe-light* to make their activity look all the more frenetic. [NOTE: The Beast will *not* engage in this activity until *after* he has made his first apearance in the show; we want to save his physical shock-value as a surprise.] The set *must* be changed (i.e.: walls shifted, furniture properly placed, any "found-onstage-as-new-scene-begins" personnel in their proper places) during MAXINE's dance and be ready for action the moment she exits; *not* at the moment her music ceases, or we lose the fun of her slump-shuffle exit. Only when she is fully offstage do stage lights COME UP FULL, and play-action recommences.

In brief, then, here is what happens, lighting-wise:

A) Current scene finishes, B) stage lights dim to one-third as MAXINE enters downstage left, C) her INTRO

MUSIC plays, D) the next bit is all simultaneous: Spot hits MAXINE, strobe-light starts, *MAXINE does her thing* while cast/crew shift set, E) MAXINE exits, and F) stage lights come up full, and new scene starts. If done with split-second timing, these scene-shift intervals will be a *highlight* of the production rather than an *interruption,* and should provoke laughter and applause each time they occur.

3) There are only three exceptions to the MAXINE saga: Her *first* and her *last* appearance onstage [For the first scene, in which we first meet MAXINE and HARRY, there is, of course, *no* set-change occurring once her dance begins; at her *final* entrance onstage, there is *no* follow-spot and *no* alteration in the onstage lighting at all. Reasons for this will be obvious when you reach that point in the script.] and her "THEN CAME THE DAWN" crossover.

THE AUTHOR

Beauty and the Beast. Really.

ACT ONE

OVERTURE ENDS. STAGE LIGHTS COME UP ONE-THIRD. Sign on easel reads "BEAUTY AND THE BEAST. REALLY." Farm set is in place, with poolside-type lounge chair just right of center. (NOTE: The set-sketch of the two sets indicates only the necessities. You may also have a butter churn, hay bale, or whatever else you want — and are able to clear, fast — in the farm scenes, and rich draperies, knickknacks, oil paintings, chandelier, etc. in the castle set.) Stage is empty. From offstage L., *we hear:*

MAXINE. (*off*) Ooh, Harry, that's my cue! What'll I do?!

HARRY. (*off*) Get out on the *stage,* stupid!

(*MAXINE enters a few feet onstage, along with HARRY. She is in tap shoes, shorts, blouse, bolero jacket and bellcap-style hat with chinstrap; every item of clothing that lacks spangles makes up for the lack with beads and/or metallic tassels. HARRY is in a derby, checked coat, vest, bright-colored slacks, wingtip shoes and spats; he also is smoking a very large cigar.*)

MAXINE. I'm so nervous. I think I'm gonna throw up.

HARRY. (*doing a Svengali*) Nonsense! Listen, Max-

11

ine, this is your big moment, the moment you've worked for all your life! Why, the show couldn't go *on* without you! Your part is the most important in the whole play!

MAXINE. Then why don't I have any lines?

HARRY. (*a little exasperated*) Look, kid, let me explain once more, slowly: This show has two sets. Audiences hate watching people change sets. So when it's time to change the sets—*you* come on and distract them! It's an old magician's trick—misdirection. He makes you look at his left hand while his right hand is pocketing the rabbit.

MAXINE. But there's no rabbit in this show. . . ?

HARRY. Kiddo. Listen. All you got to do is get out stage center, and when you hear your music intro, start those fabulous feet tapping! The rest will be theatrical history! Trust me!

MAXINE. But what if the audience doesn't like me—?

HARRY. Baby, they will eat you up! I guarantee you, by the time this show comes to an end, you'll be beating adoring men off with a stick! Why, with the right kind of luck, you could wind up in the arms of a love-crazed millionaire!

MAXINE. (*squeals with delight*) Ooh! That's positively dreamy! But are you sure that—

HARRY. Not to worry. The overture's over. They'll start your intro in a moment. And when that curtain opens—come out tapping!

MAXINE. (*shades her eyes, peers out front*) Harry . . . *what* curtain?

HARRY. (*looks, sees audience, reacts*) Yipe! Excuse me, Baby! Break a leg! (*Turns and almost leaps offstage* L. *MAXINE stands a moment longer in wide-eyed terror, then leans gingerly toward the accompanist.*)

MAXINE. (*a nervous whisper*) Hit it!

(*MUSIC INTROS; MAXINE does her thing; while she is doing her thing, BEAUTY enters, gets onto lounge chair and leans back, placing one of those sun-reflector things under her chin and closing her eyes; when MAXINE has removed show-title card, exposing "THE FARM" card, and gone off* R., *and STAGE LIGHTS COME UP FULL, nothing happens for a moment; then LULA enters* D.R., *carrying a pair of old-fashioned wooden buckets and heads toward* UC *exit [the gap between house and barn], speaking as she trudges past BEAUTY.*)

LULA. Beauty, it's nearly ten o'clock in the morning! This is a farm! There's work to do!

HOLGA. (*emerging* UC, *carrying plate of cookies*) Now-now, Lula, the poor child can hardly work today! (*They cross paths, LULA nearing* UC *as HOLGA nears chair.*) She has an absolutely *horrible* hangnail!

LULA. (*pauses for:*) Any chance it's terminal? (*exits*)

HOLGA. Beauty—? Beauty, darling? I brought you some fresh-baked cookies!

BEAUTY. (*sits up, sets reflector aside, takes a cookie*) Why, dear Stepmother Holga—how nice of you! But then, one so beautiful as I probably *deserves* splendid treatment.

HOLGA. Let's be realistic. This cookie is not your just reward—it's a *bribe!* There's gotta be *some* way to get you off your rump and into the farm business! My daughter Lula has to do the work of *two men,* with farmhands being too scared to work a spread this near the enchanted forest. The *least* you could do is *look* busy!

BEAUTY. (*finishes cookie, dusts off her fingertips lightly, rises from chair and stretches her arms overhead*

rapturously, all in one smooth motion, on:) Oh, but
sweet Stepmother Holga, I *am* busy—day in, day out,
without pause!

HOLGA. (*incredulous*) Doing *what?!*

BEAUTY. (*hugging herself dreamily*) Why, dreaming
of the handsome young prince who will come someday
and take me away from all this horrid labor!

HOLGA. Labor? Who are you trying to kid! You not
only don't *do* any chores, you won't even watch the *rest*
of us doing them!

BEAUTY. A prince wouldn't want his sweet bride to
have ugly calluses on her dainty hands.

HOLGA. Well, if you spend much more time in that
lounge chair, let's hope he never sees your dainty
behind! (*moves to butter churn, or whatever, near front
of house, and will start working, during:*)

BEAUTY. (*has gasped in reaction to HOLGA's line*)
Stepmother Holga—your language is so *common!* If I
had a fan to fan myself, I'd feel faint, hearing such
naughty words!

HOLGA. You call *that* naughty? Honey, I've got words
I haven't even *used* yet!

BEAUTY. Well, when my prince comes along, I'll see
that *you* never are allowed to come visit me!

HOLGA. (*hard at work*) Thank heaven for small
favors! Though no prince in his right mind would ride
within a mile of this dump!

BEAUTY. (*pouts prettily*) That's all *you* know!
(*MUSIC INTROS, and she sings:*)

    Someday someone
    From some far land
    Silently will come to me
    And beg for my hand!
    Someday someone

From some far place
Shall discover that he loves
My lovely face!
He'll ride up on his mighty horse,
And seat me on his lap, of course,
Till he buys a new
Saddle for two. . . !
Yes, someday someone
From far away
Tenderly will bend his knee,
Call me his gal, and I shall say:
"Yes, my darling!",
Then buy my bridal bouquet. . . !
When someone comes from somewhere,
Someday!

(*MUSIC CONTINUES, and as BEAUTY rapturously
[oh, hell, let's save on adverb-typing: She does*
everything *rapturously, prettily, breathlessly, and
suchlike] repeats her song, HOLGA -- still hard at
work — sings a few choice sentiments of her own:*)

HOLGA.
That girl! That girl!
Her head is in a whirl
With dreams of handsome princes
Coming to woo!
Well, they're welcome to
That girl! That girl!
Inspecting ev'ry curl
While I'm preserving quinces,
Sewing chintz and baking blintzes!
There she sits all day admiring
Herself, not even once perspiring!

That girl! That girl!
As pretty as a pearl,
And just about as helpful!
She should be helping me
Do the dishes, or
Start mopping up the floor,
But no! She'd rather sit and sigh!
I'd love to dock her in Shanghai—
Knock her in the eye—
Lock her in the sty—
Or sock her with a pie—
That girl!

(*At song's finish, BEAUTY sits on chair, but does not recline, and sighs.*)

BEAUTY. Oh, Holga—whatever am I to do?
HOLGA. (*The implication isn't true, but she says it anyhow:*) For starters—shoot your singing-teacher!
BEAUTY. (*pouts*) Holga!

(*Then, from offstage* L., *we hear:*)

BEAU. (*off*) Beauty! Beauty, darling—!
BEAUTY. (*springs to her feet*) It's Beau! My own sweet swain! Oh, and I look an absolute mess! (*starts running toward* UC *exit*) He mustn't see me like this!
HOLGA. He shouldn't be seeing you at all! In case it's slipped your mind—if you have one—Beau used to be *Lula's* gentleman before I married your father and you moved into the farmhouse. Won't romping with him cramp your style if that *prince* shows up?
BEAUTY. (*pauses short of exit*) A girl has to have *someone* to practice on! (*exits*)

BEAU. (*Enters* D.L., *stops; he is your typically handsome young stalwart, long on height and muscle, short on sense.*) Good morrow to you, Dame Holga!

HOLGA. Hi there, Beau. If it's Beauty you're looking for, your little poopsie-woopsie is headed for the hairspray. I'll tell her you're here. (*picks up her finished work and heads for* UC *exit*)

BEAU. I thank you, goodwoman.

(*She exits; he looks idly about, sees the discarded sunreflector, picks it up, smiles fondly at it, cradles it to his heart, then sets it on chair; a moment later, LULA re-enters* UC, *both buckets — now empty — dangling by their bails from one hand; she sees BEAU, reacts.*)

LULA. Oh! It's you! (*hastily sets buckets down behind her*) And me such a mess! (*In her case it's true: there's a smudge on one cheek, a lock of hair dangling across her forehead, and the work apron over her dress is rumpled and stained.*)

BEAU. You look just fine, Lula.

LULA. Thank you. I know it's not true, but — thank you anyway. I — I suppose you're here to see Beauty?

BEAU. Uh . . . well . . .

LULA. Oh, don't be ashamed, Beau. She *is* lovely. No matter what *else* she may be, there's no denying she's practically spectacular in the good looks department. Men are so blind.

BEAU. That's not so.

LULA. You said I looked just fine. You *must* be blind.

BEAU. Aw, Lula, don't tease.

LULA. (*fighting unwanted tears*) Tease? Why would I tease you? A girl only teases a man she — a man she cares about — and — and if you think for a moment that I — that I feel — Oh, Beau! (*turns her face away, covers face with hands, sobs*)

BEAU. (*goes to her*) Lula, don't. You *know* I still *like* you. Don't be unhappy. Please.

LULA. (*with a bit more control*) Happiness isn't something a person *decides* to be, Beau. It's something a person *is* or *isn't!*

BEAU. Now, that's where you're wrong! Happiness isn't an event, it's an attitude! Think happy and you'll *feel* happy — feel happy and you'll *be* happy!

LULA. That's a bit difficult to do at ten-thirty in the morning on a farm. Perhaps if I were a lady of leisure, like *some* ladies I know —

BEAU. It doesn't take comfort and conveniences to be happy, Lula honey. Happiness doesn't *come* to your heart — it comes *out* of it!

LULA. (*a bit stung*) Well! Cheery as a chipmunk, aren't you! How simple you make it sound!

BEAUTY. Lula, honey, it *is* simple! (*MUSIC IN-TROS, and he sings:*)

> When you start the day with a heart that's happy,
> Trouble comes your way, but it passes through.
> If you want the sun, better make it snappy!
> When your heart has fun,
> Then the rest of you has a heyday, too!
> Let your heart go "Thump!" to a happy tempo!
> Make your worries jump! Bid 'em all goodbye!
> Trouble likes the dark, trouble likes the gloom,
> So a single spark gives ya lots of room!
> Get a heart that's happy! Have a heart and try!

LULA. (*picks up buckets, sings:*)

> Work I shouldn't stop!
> To miss a moment's not well-bred.
> Simpleminded optimism

Never made a bed!

BEAU.

But the work gets done much quicker
If your outlook's bright!

LULA.

Well, perhaps one tiny flicker
Of a smile's all right . . .
(*She smiles; BEAU laughs, casually slaps her on the
back, nearly toppling her, and goes on:*)

BEAU.

Brighten up your day with a heart that's happy!

LULA.

I don't know the way. I'm not much for mirth.

BEAU.

Try a smile like this!
(*overdoes it*)

LULA.

But it looks so sappy!

BEAU.

When you're into bliss,
Looking goofy's worth all the gold on earth!

LULA.

How can work get done if I waste time grinning?

BEAU.

Once a grin's begun, working woes depart!
So for heaven's sake, lighten up your day!
Give yourself a break! Grin your cares away!
Get a heart that's happy! Now's the time to start!
(*takes her hands, coaxing and coaching her:*)
When you start the day with a heart that's happy—

LULA. (*pulls hands free, turns back*)

Trouble comes to stay!

BEAU.

No, it passes through!
(*turns her back to face him*)

If your life's a mess, take a tip from Pappy:
When you incandesce,
Cloudy skies turn blue, and your dreams come
  true!
(*She's starting to warm up a bit, as:*)
BOTH.
  When your heartbeats lilt to a happy tempo,
  All your worries wilt, wrinkle and depart!
LULA. (*out front, growing enthused*)
  Fill your heart with cheer!
BEAU. (*out front*)
  Show your heart the light!
LULA.
  Buy your heart a beer!
BEAU.
  Make your heart burn bright!
  (*turns to her*)
  Though your teeth are gappy —
LULA. (*laughs, takes his hands*)
  Be a happy chappie!
BOTH.
  Knock your troubles sappy
  With a happy heart!

(*At song's end, they are much aware of one another, and are zeroing in for a kiss, when:*)

BEAUTY. (*off*) Yoo-hoo! Beau, darling! Where are you? (*enters* UC, *stops*) Oh, *there* you are . . . and there *she* is.

LULA. (*crushed, picks up buckets*) Don't worry your pretty little head about it. I've got to go get more water from the well. The cistern's only half-filled, and Father always likes a bath before lunch!

BEAUTY. But Father hardly *ever* eats lunch.

LULA. (*shrugs*) That might explain the way he smells.

BEAUTY. Really, Lula! Such a thing to say in front of Beau!

LULA. If *I* didn't tell him, his *nose* would! (*Then reacts as FATHER, a pleasant-visaged man of middle age, slogs wearily in from D.R. with a bridle.*) Why, there he is, now! Father! I hope you weren't thrown by your horse?!

FATHER. You shoulda hoped a little sooner, Lula. He not only throwed me, he jumped the fence and got clean away. That means I gotta do all the spring plowing by hand!

HOLGA. (*enters UC, sees him*) Oh! Darling, are you all right?

FATHER. Nothing wrong with me that a good hot bath won't fix!

LULA. Oh, dear! And I haven't finished drawing the water yet!

BEAU. Don't worry, Lula. *I'll* lend you a hand!

BEAUTY. What, wander off to the well with her, when you might be spending your time with a much lovelier person such as myself?

BEAU. Aw, but Beauty — !

BEAUTY. (*pouts, turns her back to him*) And here I was just this morning thinking, if you and I were ever to marry, what with you being so marvelously handsome and me being so fantastically lovely, just *think* of the absolutely *beautiful* little *children* we two could adopt!

BEAU. *Adopt?!*

BEAUTY. (*faces him*) Well, Beau, you *know* what having one's *own* babies does to a girl's figure! Besides, which would you rather look at, screaming little tots or ravishing little me?

BEAU. Well, if you put it that way — Hey, what'd you mean, just now, *if* you and I get married? *I* thought it was just about all *settled.*

BEAUTY. Oh, but Beau, handsome as you are, you are hardly *rich* enough for someone such as I. I need luxury, and comfort, and a life of ease.

HOLGA. I guess *I* can vouch for *that!*

BEAU. (*stands tall*) Okay. Okay, if that's what it takes to win you — I'm going to go off and seek my fortune and *get* rich! *Then* will you marry me?

BEAUTY. *How* rich will you *be?*

BEAU. Extremely!

BEAUTY. Then of *course* I'll marry you, Beau! (*He reaches for her gleefully; she backs off.*) Not now. Then.

BEAU. (*turns, faces* R) Then I'm *off* through the enchanged forest to seek my fortune!

HOLGA. Oh, no!

FATHER. You mustn't!

LULA. *Not* through an enchanted *forest!*

BEAUTY. It could be *dreadfully* dangerous!

BEAU. Aw, that enchanted stuff is just a lot of old wives' tales!

OTHERS. Ha! That's all *you* know!

(*MUSIC INTROS, and:*)

BEAUTY.
    We've a customary mouse,
    And an ordinary cat
    Of an unexciting pedigree.
LULA.
    In my customary blouse
    And my ordinary hat,
    Clothing's unexciting as can be.

HOLGA.
  We've a customary house
  On our ordinary farm
  Near an unexciting waterway.
FATHER.
  With my customary spouse
  On my ordinary arm
  We live unexciting lives all day.
ALL FOUR.
  In our day-to-day existence
  There is nothing odd or strange.
  But the moment night has fallen
  There's one teensy-weensy change!
  And so, we . . .
  (*Tune has been bright and pleasant; now it becomes ominous, and rather terrifying, on:*)
  Never go into the wood,
  Where horrid atrocities loom!
BEAUTY.
  An innocent ditch may be hiding a witch
  Who will give you a hitch on her broom!
ALL FOUR.
  Just one little walk in the wood
  Could be curiosity's tomb!
LULA.
  Where the siren decoys and the monster destroys
  And the flowers have poison perfume!
FATHER.
  One man I knew thought all the rumors
  Were a flight of fancy!
  He ran into a fairy there who
  Turned him into a pansy!
ALL FOUR.
  Never go into the wood,
  Where dark animosities bloom!

How can you survive where the trees are alive
And they're always conniving your doom?
HOLGA.
One man astride his donkey spied
A harmless-looking flagon;
He drained the cup, and when he looked up,
He found his ass a dragon!
ALL FOUR.
Never go into the wood
Where monsters will make you their mark!
BEAUTY.
There's a bogeyman there
With a head like a bear!
LULA.
There's a goblin who tracks
People down with an axe!
HOLGA.
There's a troll and a ghoul!
FATHER.
So don't stroll like a fool—
ALL FOUR.
Through the wood in the dangerous dark. . . !
(*then tune lightens, for:*)
Though in daylight it's rather a lark!

(*On final beat of accompaniment, ALL FOUR give a unified shrug of dismissive disinterest.*)

BEAU. Aha! It's daylight now! I can be beyond the enchanted forest in six hours' walking!
LULA. But sunset comes in *five* hours.
BEAU. (*hesitates; then:*) I'll walk faster! (*exits* R.)
BEAUTY. Well, it's time for my beauty-sleep! (*heads houseward*)

HOLGA. If sleeping makes you beautiful, no wonder she's a looker!

FATHER. Wait, Beauty, I'll come with you! You can tell me about your day.

HOLGA. (*as FATHER and BEAUTY exit* UC) *That* oughta kill five minutes.

LULA. Oh, Mother, I'm *so* worried about Beau, out in that woods!

HOLGA. (*concerned*) Don't worry, honey. He'll be fine. And — look — forget about the trip to the well. I'll tell your stepfather he smells just fine, and you can break for lunch, okay?

LULA. How can I eat when I'm overmastered by fear and apprehension?

HOLGA. Lula — I hate to remind you, but — that's *another* woman's boyfriend you're getting worked up over . . . I mean . . . you *heard* what he said . . . (*gets no reply; withdraws tactfully*) I'll just -- go see about that lunch. (*exits* UC)

LULA. (*sighs, looks at buckets she holds, then deliberately tosses them onto chair*) Try sitting on *those* for awhile, my fine stepsister! Though with both of them under your bustle, no one would notice any difference! (*stops*) No. No, that's not true. She has a lovely figure — and a lovely face — and a lovely voice, too. Oh, but — (*wrings her hands piteously*) *What* in the world does that man *see* in her?! (*MUSIC INTROS, and she sings:*)

> I can't cope in her class,
> Common sense decrees.
> Who could hope to surpass
> All her qualities?
>
> She's lovely
> As any girl has a right to be,

So why does my heart tell me
He ought to be mine?
She's lovely,
With charms impossible to resist,
So why does my heart insist
He ought to be mine?
I could never offer two eyes
Blue as skies in summer!
But it's such a bummer
That he doesn't love me!
Oh, she's so lovely
That someone plainer but just as sweet
Simply cannot compete
With someone so fine
In her depressing loveliness!
Something
In her has made his heart sing . . .
And so, their love must be fate's design . . .
But he ought to be mine. . . !

(*At song's end, she covers her face and weeps; while she
is weeping, SAM enters; SAM is a hound dog of
rather large size [after all, he's a full-grown man in a
dog costume], who should look as much like
Beauregard Bugleboy of the old* Pogo *comic strip as
possible; he enters on all fours, but when occasion
permits, he also ambulates upright on two legs;
right now, he moves to our weeping LULA, and
rubs his cheek amiably against the side of her leg.*)

SAM. Wurf. (*Do* not *bark; say "Wurf."*)
LULA. (*sees him, sniffs away her tears, starts stooping
down, hugging him, rubbing his ears, etc.*) Oh, Sam!

How nice it is to have a friend like you! You *never* judge people by their looks, just by their smell!

(*As proof of this, FATHER re-enters* UC, *SAM gives a sniff in his direction, howls mournfully, and scurries to — we presume — an upwind spot* R. *of the chair; BEAUTY and HOLGA re-enter* UC *during:*)

FATHER. Lula, don't play with that old fleabag! You'll be scratching so bad we'll have to dunk you in the sheep-dip!

HOLGA. Now-now, don't pick on old Sam! He'll be the only protection us helpless womenfolk will have while you're gone.

LULA. Gone? Father, are you going somewhere?

FATHER. I fear so, Lula. With my plowhorse run away, we're gonna need some money, and a fella in the city owes me a bundle. I hafta journey there and get it, so we can buy a new horse.

HOLGA. Say, while you're there, you can pick me up a few things, if you would.

FATHER. Be glad to, Holga. But I'd better write 'em down, or I'll forget. (*gets pad and pencil from pocket*)

BEAUTY. Father, do you know how *long* you'll be away?

FATHER. Well, lemme see . . . it takes pretty near one week to walk the long way, around the enchanted forest — and another week to walk back.

BEAUTY. Oh, what a shame! And my birthday's in just eight more days!

FATHER. Shucks, I plumb forgot! Well, tell you what — I can *go* the long way, then take the shortcut *through* the enchanted forest to come back. That'll get me here right on time!

LULA. Oh, but that's so dangerous! It isn't worth the peril!

BEAUTY. To get here on time for my birthday? Of course it is!

FATHER. Let's not start any arguments! I've got to get to the city, get that money, do some business negotiating for grain and feed, and get back here, all in eight days! Now, what is it you want me to pick up for you, Holga?

HOLGA. (*looks ruefully at peasant gown*) Well, I could certainly use some new clothes.

LULA. And *I* could use some jewelry. It's not that I'm a spendthrift, but when a girl's as plain-looking as I am, she needs something to catch a fella's eye.

FATHER. Okay, clothes and jewelry. And how about you, Beauty?

BEAUTY. Oh, why bother? After all, when my prince comes along, I shall have everything luxurious in rich abundance.

FATHER. But you *must* want *something?*

BEAUTY. Oh — well — perhaps — a flower.

FATHER. That's *it?!*

BEAUTY. I wouldn't want *more* than one. After all, it's bad enough making *one* flower look drab beside *my* glorious good looks.

HOLGA. Oh, but, husband — what with the journey and the meetings and all, are you sure you'll have the *time* for the other things?

FATHER. Don't see why not. (*MUSIC INTROS, and he sings:*)

When my bus'ness meetings stop,
There'll be time enough to shop
Just before I start the tricky journey back.

So, for each of you, my dears,
I shall buy some souvenirs.
Let me write down each particular you lack.

HOLGA.

Rich new clothing would be nice.

LULA.

Or some jew'lry of great price.

BEAUTY.

Almost any little flower
You can bring me will suffice.

FATHER. (*poises pencil over pad*)

I may forget the details
By the time I get to town.
Be a little more specific
While I write your wishes down.

(*spoken:*) What do you want? (*and he will commence
writing as the ladies commence singing with great enthusiasm:*)

HOLGA.

A velvet hat with a feathery plume!

LULA.

A ruby so big it lights up the room!

FATHER.

A hat and ruby, that's two—
Now, Beauty, how about you?

BEAUTY.

Oh, well, perhaps a tiny rosebud
Coming into bloom!

HOLGA.

Say, while you're at it, some new silken hose!

LULA.

Some golden rings for my fingers and toes!

FATHER.

Hat, ruby, rings, hose—that's four,
So Beauty needs something more.

BEAUTY.
   Oh, no, dear Father,
   Please don't bother!
   Just a simple rose!
FATHER.
   But surely, Beauty, you want more than that?
   New dress, new shoes, new coat, new hat?
HOLGA/LULA.
   Oh, let the poor girl be,
   And concentrate on me!
BEAUTY.
   For me, a simple rose is where it's at!
FATHER. (*shrugs*)
   Well, that is that!
   (*starts to put pad away, but must write some more,
   with exasperation, as:*)
HOLGA.
   Except a gown with a nice ermine trim!
LULA.
   An em'rald pendant to make my head swim!
FATHER.
   Three kinds of jew'lry and clothes;
   But, Beauty, don't you suppose—?
BEAUTY.
   Oh, no, just pluck a simple rose
   From any handy limb!
FATHER. (*rechecking what he's written*)
   Let's see now:
   Ruby, em'rald, golden rings,
   A feathered hat, a gown, silk hose . . .
HOLGA/LULA.
   Such lovely and expensive things!
BEAUTY.
   And just one inexpensive rose!

FATHER. (*starts closing pad*)
   One red rose.
BEAUTY.
   Make it white.
FATHER.
   White?
   (*but he recommences writing, during:*)
BEAUTY.
   And not a thorn in sight.
FATHER. (*sarcastically*)
   From bush or tree?
BEAUTY. (*oblivious to his irony*)
   From creeping vines.
FATHER.
   But vines have spines like porcupines!
BEAUTY.
   When you find its bed . . .
FATHER.
   I'm running out of lead!
BEAUTY. (*waxing enthusiastic*)
   It should be
   Not too large, not too small,
   Clinging to a granite wall,
   Part in sun, part in shade,
   Fast to blossom, slow to fade,
   Not too moist, not too dry—
FATHER. (*backing uneasily toward* D.L. *exit*)
   Look, I've really got to fly—
LULA.
   Remember my jewels!
HOLGA.
   Remember my clothes!
BEAUTY.
   And your little unselfish

Beauty, who chose—
FATHER. (*nodding grimly as he pockets pad*)
Just one white, thornless, granite-climbing—
FATHER/HOLGA.
Semi-shaded, quickly-blooming—
FATHER/HOLGA/LULA.
Never-fading, dryly dampish—
ALL FOUR.
Simple little rose!

(*FATHER shakes his head in disbelief, and exits even as
MUSIC is finishing, and SAM hurries to stand two-
legged beside the three women, and all four of them
wave goodbye to the exiting FATHER, in exaggerated flutter-fingered unison. Then MUSIC IN-
TROS, and MAXINE does her thing, and the castle
set is in place by the time she flips the card over to
its "THE CASTLE" side and exits; LIGHTS
COME UP on castle set; the garden doors R. are
open, the table is laid with a sumptuous dinner for
one, and we can see at least one white rose half-
poking through open window [this is a frame only,
with no sash or shutters or panes] U.R. on a vine;
after a moment, FATHER appears rather nervously
in doorway, peeks cautiously into room, and:*)

FATHER. (*will move to UC corridor arch, very slowly,
in a kind of nervous-exploratory start-stop fashion, during:*) Hello? . . . Anybody home? . . . I lost my way in
the forest, and night is falling, and I saw your light, so
. . . (*stops and there comes a terrifying ROAR*) Yipe!
Perhaps . . . I'd be safer in the *forest*—! (*is backing
from arch toward doors R. as he speaks, then turns and

rushes doorward on:) In fact, I'm sure I would! (*Both doors SLAM shut just before he gets there.*) Oh, no! I'm trapped! Helpless! And alone! (*We hear an even LOUDER ROAR.*) Well, maybe not *quite* alone. . . ! (*rushes to bed, drops prone along its D side, to conceal himself from whatever is coming through that archway, covers his face, trembles*) Me and my stupid *shortcuts!*

(*MUSIC INTROS the ominous "Entrance of The Beast" theme, and we see a misshapen shadow upon the center of the wall U of archway, growing larger as the music grows louder—and then the BEAST springs into view from area left of archway and lands dead center there, facing down into room; he is fearsome indeed, with the snout of a pig, ears like a bat, and a short upcurving horn in the middle of his forehead [this is a rubber mask, the sort that covers the head from the mouth upward, so that* real *lower lip and chin are free for talking and singing]; besides this, he has a shaggy mane of hair, hands as hairy and taloned as a bear's [simply cotton gardening gloves with glued-on fuzz and false fingernails], and wears cavalier boots, tights and a tunic, all under a large dark cloak; his leap into view is simultaneous with last horrible chord of intro, and then as music becomes fast and frightening, he strides here and there [looking under table, into bureau drawers, out window, etc.; everywhere but where FATHER is hiding, of course], his movements alternating between manly stride and bestial scuttle; he will find FATHER immediately after final chord of song. That is the sequence of events. Now, as to the lyrics:*)

BEAST. (*off; during "Entrance of the Beast" theme, spoken:*)
There's a fear-smell in the gloom,
But no person am I seeing!
Still, I think I can assume
It's a tasty human being! . . .
(*now leaps into view with ROAR, then — over the now-rapid music pace, ROARS MORE RHYTHMI-CALLY:*)
Guh-RAAA! . . .Guh-ROOO!
Oh, what I'm gonna do!
(*sings as he commences ferocious search:*)
    Somebody is hiding in my castle!
FATHER. (*will let us see his fear-drawn face, now, till end of song, as he begins his interjected whimpers:*)
Who is *he?!*
BEAST.
    Somebody is cowering with fear!
FATHER. He must mean *me!*
BEAST.
    I'll find his hiding-place—
FATHER. Oh, woe!
BEAST.
    And meet him face-to-face—
FATHER. Low blow!
BEAST.
    And make him squeal,
    And shortly he'll
    Be gone without a trace!

(*shouts simultaneously*)

BEAST. Ho! Ho! Ho!   FATHER. No! No! No!

BEAST.

When I find who's hiding in my castle —

FATHER. Dear-oh-dear!

BEAST.

I am gonna make him disappear!

FATHER. He's almost here!

BEAST.

His bones I'm gonna crunch!

FATHER. Oh, why?!

BEAST.

His toes I'm gonna munch!

FATHER. Oh, my!

BEAST. (*at foot of bed, about to peer toward FATHER*)

He ought to make a lovely lunch!

FATHER. (*over final chords of song*) I just could die!

BEAST. (*sees him*) Ah-HAAAA! (*leans over him, talons outstretched*)

FATHER. (*pops up to his knees, pivots to face BEAST, then — all in one movement -- sits back on heels, clasps hands before chest, shuts eyes . . . and then babbles:*) Oh, don't eat me, *please* don't eat me, have some mercy, I'm an old man, you wouldn't like me, I meant no harm, I'm sorry I intruded, I simply lost my way, spare me, spare me, spare me!

BEAST. (*shrugs, stands straight, unflexes talons*) Okay, you're spared.

FATHER. (*half-opens eyes, squinting at him*) Just like that? Why?

BEAST. I only eat *red* meat — and *you* are obviously a *chicken!*

FATHER. (*flops forward, grabbing BEAST's ankles, kissing the toes of his boots*) Oh, thank you, thank you, thank you!

BEAST. Hey, cut it out, I just *polished* those boots!

FATHER. (*stops immediately, and scurries backward on knees till bedside wall stops him, and gets shakily to his feet, all during:*) Oh, of course! A thousand pardons, your grace! Your highness! Your majesty! Your beastliness!

BEAST. *Enough!*

FATHER. Oh, yes sir! Just as you say! Whatever you say! Anything you say!

BEAST. And I say, *"Enough!"* Cease this incessant babbling! (*FATHER shuts up, remains tensely against wall.*) That's better. Now, tell me — what are you doing here?

FATHER. Well, you see, tomorrow is my daughter Beauty's birthday, and I've been away at the city, and to get back in time, I left early this morning to shortcut through the enchanted forest, but the paths were very strange, and I lost my way, and darkness had started to fall, and —

BEAST. You're *babbling* again!

FATHER. Oh. I'm sorry. Terribly sorry. Most frightfully sorry. Most totally and extremely sorry —! (*BEAST gives a low, soft rumble of incipient roar.*) I'll stop. There, I've stopped. Not another word. Quiet as a corpse — oh, dear — I mean, quiet as a mouse — a very small mouse —

BEAST. (*Holds up hand; FATHER goes silent, cringes.*) There. That's it. Calm. Peace. Quiet. You say you have journeyed the forest since dawn?

FATHER. Yes, sir.

BEAST. Then you must be very hungry. There is dinner laid out at the table there. Sit and eat. And then you must rest the night in this bed before you continue your journey in the morning.

FATHER. Why—that is most generous of you, sir! But—and I know I'm sticking my neck out for asking it, but—*why* have you decided to spare me?

BEAST. I only eat bandits and robbers who prowl these woods. I thought you to be one of them. But you are obviously a family man, with a child—

FATHER. *Two* childs!—children. Beauty and Lula. And I have a wife, a goodwoman named Holga. And a dog named Sam. And a nice little farm, and—! Oh, dear. I'm babbling again.

BEAST. Yes, and the longer you talk, the hungrier I get! Don't press your luck!

FATHER. Yes, sir! I mean, no, sir! I mean—I'll be quiet. I won't open my mouth again tonight. Oh, except when I have dinner, of course. I mean, I'd *have* to open my mouth to *eat*, and—(*BEAST starts growling again.*) Sorry.

BEAST. (*strides to arch, turns*) Eat well. Sleep well. Then be on your way in the morning.

FATHER. You *got* it! (*BEAST exits* L. *via archway-corridor; FATHER gasps in relief, fans his brow, then moves up to table, sits in chair, lifts knife and fork.*) It certainly looks delicious! I wonder what kind of *meat* this is? (*thinks that one over*) On second thought, maybe I'm better off not knowing!

(*Starts plying knife and fork; MUSIC INTROS, and MAXINE does her thing; this time, however, she carries a wide card on which we see "THEN CAME THE DAWN . . ." and tosses it offstage* R. *so she can do her usual finish beside easel, but she does not, of course, change the card there; during her dance, table will be cleared of food and china and cutlery, and FATHER will get into bed; then when*

MAXINE exits and LIGHTS COME BACK TO FULL: FATHER sighs, mumbles, then abruptly wakens and sits up.)

FATHER. Oh! Where am I? . . . Oh, yes, now I remember! (*shivers, gets out of bed*) I'd best be on my way. I hope all my bundles and packages are still outside in the garden where I left them . . . (*Steps toward doors; when he is almost at them, they swing open by themselves; he peeks out.*) Oh, good, they've been undisturbed. Which is more than I can say for *me!* Oh, but if *only* I had been able to get that one simple rose my darling Beauty wanted. But the white roses I found weren't thornless, the thornless ones had no smell, the sweet-smelling ones—(*stops as he espies rose at window*) Why—of all the marvelous luck! There is the very rose Beauty requested! White—thornless—on a vine—delightfully sweet-smelling—part in sun, part in shade—and even growing on a granite wall! What incredible *luck!* (*Plucks rose; immediately we hear that ROAR again.*) —incredible *bad* luck! I'd better get *out* of here! (*Rushes for doors; they slam in his face again.*) Oh, no! Oh, dear! Oh, help! Help!

BEAST. (*leaping into view in archway as before*) *No one* can help you! So *this* is how you repay my kindness, my mercy, my generosity! Stealing one of my prize roses! Well, this time—bandit or not—you shall grace my table tonight!

FATHER. (*falls on his knees*) No, please! Don't eat me! Not that! Anything but that!

BEAST. *Any*thing. . . ?!

FATHER. Well . . . anything within *reason*. . . !

(*MUSIC INTROS, and:*)

BEAST. (*sings*)
　　Let me see, now, I could torture you
　　On the rack, and just distort your two
　　Shoulders till they won't support your cravat!
　　Whatta ya think o' that?
FATHER. (*will get cautiously to his feet as he sings:*)
　　I'd prefer a somewhat milder approach!
　　Let's say a nasty smile or a
　　Chuckle as you crushed the pile of my hat!
　　Whatta ya think o' that?
BEAST.
　　No-no, my friend,
　　Such methods just won't do!
　　'Cause I intend
　　To tenderly dismember you!
FATHER.
　　Isn't there some sweet alternative?
　　I don't wish to break or burn or give
　　Screaming comments just to furnish you fun!
　　Really, I gotta run!
BEAST.
　　I'll tell you what:
　　Suppose we make a deal?
　　It's milder, but
　　It might provide me with a meal!
　　(*extends hand*)
FATHER. (*after a split-second hesitation, shakes his hand*)
　　It's a deal! It can't be worse than
　　The rack!
BEAST.
　　Just send to me the person
　　Who's first to greet you when you're
　　Mercif'ly free!

FATHER.
That will be my poor dog Sam,
But I shall agree!
The oncoming beat of his feet
Will be sweet as he's greeting me!
(*Doors magically open; he starts for them.*)
He isn't vicious!
BEAST.
In a nice soufflé
He'll be delicious!
FATHER. (*in doorway, now, facing back into room*)
He'll be here today!
BEAST.
Dogs are nutritious
To a true gourmet!
FATHER. (*with an amiable wave*)
I'm on my way!

(*He exits; BEAST laugh-growls horribly, rubbing his
hands together, heads for arch, then pauses there,
facing out front, for:*)

BEAST. His faithful dog Sam, first to greet him! (*gives
roar of fiendish laughter*) That's all *he* knows!

(*Exits* L. *via corridor, chuckling; MUSIC INTROS and
MAXINE does her thing; by the time she's flipped
card over to "THE FARM" side, and made her exit,
BEAUTY is back in chair with sun-reflector, LULA
just entering* D.R. *with filled buckets, and HOLGA
doing some kind of work near house, as LIGHTS
COME UP FULL, and:*)

LULA. (*en route to exit* UC) Beauty, I could *really* use a hand, you know!

BEAUTY. What? But today is my birthday! No one as lovely as I should work on a birthday!

HOLGA. And what's your alibi the *other* three-hundred-sixty-four days of the year?

LULA. Don't ask—she's got a million of 'em!

(*Is just about to complete her exit when SAM comes bounding in, "Wurfing" elatedly; he scurries to* C.R. *area, jumps to his two feet, pants loudly, points off into "forest" [the general offstage* R. *area], jumps up and down, etc. etc.*)

BEAUTY. Why—whatever is the matter with Sam? (*will rise and discard reflector, during:*)

LULA. (*Sets buckets out of our view* U *of house wall, moves down toward BEAUTY, all three women staring off* R. *in curiosity, during:*) There must be somebody coming!

HOLGA. (*moving to join them*) Out of the enchanted forest?! Then hadn't we better run into the house and lock all the doors and windows?!

LULA. Now, that's what I call a terrific idea!

BEAUTY. (*As they move toward* UC, *rushes ahead of them, on:*) Last one in is a monster's lunch!

FATHER. (*off*) Halooo! Anybody home there? Sam? Where are you, Sam? Come on, Sam boy! It's your lord and master, home at last!

SAM. (*evincing excitement—jumping up and down, running in circles, whatever*) Wurf! Wurf! Wurf!

BEAUTY. It's Father!

HOLGA. With my new clothes!

LULA. With my jewels!

BEAUTY. And my simple little rose! (*All three move toward forest as FATHER enters, with arms filled with packages.*)

FATHER. Sam! Sam, come greet me, boy! (*SAM pants happily, hurries toward him — then stops, holds his nose, shakes his head, runs to hide behind the women.*) Damn! I *knew* I should've taken a *bath* this morning! (*sees women approaching, drops packages in fright*) No, wait! Stay away! Don't touch me! Sam first! (*He dodges this way and that, using the chair as a barrier between him and them, but BEAUTY abruptly leaps over the chair and flings her arms around his neck.*)

BEAUTY. Father, dearest! Welcome home! *Sam* may be sensitive, but *I* don't care *what* you smell like!

FATHER. (*out front, in quiet despair*) Horse manure!

BEAUTY. (*releases him, steps back, smiles uncertainly*) Well — yes — but I *never* would have *said* so!

FATHER. (*sinks woefully onto chair, his head in his hands*) Oh, this is dreadful, catastrophic! My darlings — I have the most terrible *news* for you all!

HOLGA. They didn't have my size in clothing?

LULA. They didn't have jewelry you could afford?

BEAUTY. You couldn't pick me one stinking rose?!

FATHER. What? . . . Oh, that! . . . Here! (*takes rose from inside jacket, hands it over*) Smell it in good health — while it lasts.

BEAUTY. Oh, but surely this rose will last a long time.

FATHER. But your good health won't. (*stands wearily*) You see, dearest darling — there's something you should know . . .

BEAUTY. Oooh! Is it a birthday surprise?!

FATHER. Oh — I guess you could *call* it that, yes!

BEAUTY. What is it! Tell me! I'm just *dying* to know! Simply *dying!*

FATHER. (*nods resignedly*) That's the operative word, all right.

LULA. Father, what do you mean?

HOLGA. Yes, what are you trying to say?

FATHER. Well, the fact of the matter is — I've promised a monstrous Beast that he could have Beauty for dinner tonight.

BEAUTY. Oh. Well — if the menu's up to par — I guess I wouldn't mind dining with him — for a little while.

FATHER. I don't think you get it, Beauty. You *are* the dinner!

BEAUTY. What a terrible thing to promise! (*to LULA*) How could Father *do* such a thing! *Why* would he do it?

LULA. Actually — *I* can think of a *million* reasons!

FATHER. It wasn't my fault! I merely promised him the first one who would greet me on my return. I thought it would be Sam! (*SAM stands up on two feet, in obvious resentment, gives a growl, then starts barking and drops to all fours, chasing FATHER around the chair, during:*) Sam! Stop! There wasn't anything *personal* in it!

BEAUTY. Get him! Get him!

HOLGA. You *know* we can't run as fast as Sam!

BEAUTY. I wasn't talking to you — I was talking to Sam! All my gorgeous loveliness — covered with ketchup! (*starts to cry*)

FATHER. Beauty, please don't cry! (*Then he stops running in relief, as LULA manages to stop SAM with a deft flying tackle.*)

LULA. Now, Sam, you stay still, or I'll *never* rub your ears *again!*

FATHER. (*seeing SAM has subsided, takes out notepad, tears off a sheet and extends it*) Here, Beauty — I've written down the directions to his castle.

BEAUTY. (*ceases weeping immediately*) Castle? You mean he doesn't live in a smelly animal's lair?

FATHER. Oh, no. He seems quite wealthy — dresses splendidly — serves only the finest wines — and his silverware is solid gold!

BEAUTY. Well, why didn't you *say* so! Lula, hurry, get my bags!

LULA. (*makes false start for* UC, *then turns back*) Don't you want to *pack* them first?

HOLGA. She *keeps* them packed. Didn't want to waste any time if that *prince* came along.

LULA. Oh. (*exits*)

FATHER. Beauty — aren't you afraid?

BEAUTY. Mmmm — no, I'm not. After all, a Beast who appreciates the finer things in life would simply never eat anyone so fine as I!

HOLGA. Boy, talk about ego-trips!

LULA. (*re-enters with two small carpetbags*) Well, here they are, kiddo. *Bon voyage!*

BEAUTY. Are they very heavy, Lula?

LULA. (*hefts them, considering*) No, not bad at all.

BEAUTY. Oh, good. I wouldn't want you to get too tired carrying them.

LULA. What?! Now hold on! If you think I'm traveling *with* you —

BEAUTY. But you must, Lula! Don't you see? Every fine lady has her own handmaiden. This way, as soon as he sees us coming, he will be impressed, and perhaps allow you to join me!

LULA. On the barbecue spit?! No way, José!

BEAUTY. But — if I *don't* make a good first impression, he may *eat* me! Would you want a ghastly thing like *that* on your conscience?

LULA. Uh—well—I guess—oh, shucks, if you put it *that* way—! (*looks toward parents*) I guess I'll have to go along.

FATHER. The enchanted forest is dangerous. You should take Sam along, too, for protection. (*SAM instantly, on two feet, goes all coy and flattered and embarrassed, lowering face, twisting body left and right, etc.*)

HOLGA. Sam? Are you kidding? Sam's afraid of his own shadow! How could *he* protect the girls?

FATHER. If they meet a monster on the way, they could let him eat Sam! (*and SAM comes up behind him and kicks him square in the seat of the pants*) Ouch!

LULA. Oh, Sam—please—you have such a sensitive nose—you could smell danger coming, and warn us in time! (*SAM goes all coy, etc., again.*)

HOLGA. There, it's all settled! Good luck, girls! Drop us a postcard when you're all settled in at the castle.

FATHER. Holga, it's been a long wearisome journey— how about rustling up some ham and eggs?

HOLGA. Oh, of course, darling! Bye-bye, girls!

FATHER. You'd better hurry, so you make it before dark! (*FATHER and HOLGA exit* UC.)

LULA. (*dryly*) I hate these sad and sentimental farewells. (*hefts bags again*) Well, come on, your ladyship, let's hit the road while there's still some sunlight left!

BEAUTY. Oh, Lula—do you suppose that the Beast is actually a handsome prince under an enchantment, and that his love for me will be able to break the spell, and we can live happily ever after?

LULA. Wow! When you daydream, you daydream big! Not that I don't hope you're *right*, of course!

BEAUTY. Well, what's wrong with dreaming of a handsome prince — of the things he'll say — of the things he'll do!

LULA. Such as what?

BEAUTY. Really, Lula! A lady would never *say* such things out *loud!* It's fun to think them — but using such words is another matter entirely. Don't *you* ever dream of a handsome lover — and what he'll say — and what he'll do?

LULA. Every night, like clockwork! What red-blooded girl doesn't!

BEAUTY. Tell you what — it would make fun-conversation between here and the Beast's castle if we *shared* some of our dreamy notions!

LULA. But how *can* we? I mean, if we don't put any of the *good* stuff into *words* — ?!

BEAUTY. I have it! Whenever we get to the *good* stuff, instead of using language unsuited to a proper young lady — we'll simply say "tra-la!"

LULA. Stepsister — you've got yourself a deal!

(*MUSIC INTROS, and they start a happy stroll, their movements almost like gliding to a waltz at a skating rink — a glide here, a pirouette there, etc. [During this number — which will end as they exit* D.R. *into the enchanted forest — they can move about the farmyard, descend into the audience and go up one aisle and down the other, etc., always moving and gesturing in unison — and for comic effect, SAM can follow on two legs, wherever they go, and mimic their movements] As intro comes to its end:*)

BOTH. (*sing*)
　He'll be so grand!
　He'll smile as he tells me,
　"Tra-la, tra-la, tra-la, tra-la!"
　Then he'll take my ha-and
　And swear love compels me to
　Tra-la-la tra-la-la!
　And when we're to-
　Gether in the starry night,
　It's then he will
　Tell me I'm his heart's delight,
　And tra-lalala-lalala,
　While tra-lalala-lalala,
　As the moon comes out,
　And we shout, "Tra-la-la!"
BEAUTY.
　It's driving me frantic
　To yearn for his kiss!
LULA.
　But, oh, so romantic
　To burn with such bliss —
BOTH.
　As he whispers that
　He and I
　Are destined forever to
　Tra-la-la, tra-la, tra-la,
　As we softly si-igh
　That we will endeavor to
　Tra-lala-lalala!
　Of course, we won't
　Tra-la-la unless he uses
　Force, because tra-la-la's
　A special cruise

Upon the sea of bright romance,
So, though we love to hear his pants,
We can tra-la-la, tra-la-la
Later on, but right now,
Let's just dance!

BEAUTY.
Tra-la! Merely dance!

LULA.
Tra-la! Till we—

BOTH.
Tra-lala-lalala la-lala-lalala-la!
Tra-la!

(*They have exited* D.R. *on final note, SAM following, and are gone; a moment later, FATHER and HOLGA enter* UC, *gaze silently forestward, then sigh.*)

FATHER. Well. That's it. They've gone.

HOLGA. It'll be strange. Here on the farm. Without them.

FATHER. Of course, we always knew they'd leave us. Someday.

HOLGA. We knew it—but we didn't really believe it in our hearts.

FATHER. I guess this is something every parent goes through.

HOLGA. Yes. I guess it is.

(*FATHER places an arm fondly across her shoulders; MUSIC INTROS, and:*)

BOTH.
Happy childhood days are through.

Call their names, there's no reply
From the children that we knew
In days gone by . . .

HOLGA.

No more footsteps on the stair.

FATHER.

Tiny beds are empty, too.

HOLGA.

Nevermore will they be there.

BOTH.

What can we do? . . .
(*BOTH look about to cry, now.*)
Well . . . there's . . .
(*then MUSIC picks up to a mad cancan-tempo, and they dance — singly-then-doubly-then-singly- etc. — about the stage as they sing joyously:*)
Always Paris and the *Champs Elysees!*
Now that the kids are away,
We're gonna fly!
It would've
Been embarrassing to go on a spree
With them at home, but now we
Can touch the sky!

HOLGA.

For fear the kiddies would stare,
We lived *la vie ordinaire!*
The doctrine of *laissez-faire*
Was not for we!

FATHER.

As for the *Folies Bergeres,*
We were ashamed to go there!
But with no kids —

BOTH.

C'est la guerre! C'est la vie!

HOLGA.
    We're gonna share a *chansonette* on the Seine,
    And drink a lot of champagne!
    Is that a crime?
FATHER.
    We'll drink and dance till the dawn,
    Then raise our glasses and yawn—

(*BOTH stop dancing and raise imaginary glasses in a
    toast, for:*)

BOTH.
    "The kids are gone—and it's about time!"

(*MUSIC continues as they dance briefly up to* UC-*exit
    area, where HOLGA pulls out a small overnight
    bag for each of them, and then—each holding a
    bag—they dance* DC *to face out front, as they pick
    up the song again:*)

HOLGA.
    I'll have my hair assembled
    By the House of Dior!
FATHER.
    I'll eat *escargots* galore!
BOTH.
    We'll have a blast!
    Then more champagne we will chill,
    To toast again to the thrill—
    (*They will high-kick out front, but also move
    sideways toward* D.L. *area—inner arms across each
    other's shoulders, outer arms waving those
    overnight bags—as they finish:*)

Of having chil-
Dren
Gone
At
Last. . . . !

(*And, sustaining final note, they high-kick off* D.L.
*MUSIC gallops merrily to its finish, and then stage
lights dim to total black simultaneously with house
lights coming up full—amid* much *applause, of
course!*)

END OF ACT ONE

ACT TWO

During intermission, card is flipped to its "THE CASTLE" side, and set altered accordingly, with two additions: There is a foldable Army cot — folded — leaning against the U.R. corner below the window, and a sleeping bag — rolled up — atop the bureau (or dresser, or whatever sort of multi-drawered bedroom fixture you use). ENTR'ACTE ends. LIGHTS COME UP FULL. After a moment, BEAUTY enters through open doors, cautiously, and moves a few paces into room; then LULA — empty handed — enters similarly till she is just behind BEAUTY; then SAM — wearily toting both carpetbags — shuffles in on two feet, shoulders slumped, and stands behind the women, panting.

BEAUTY. Well — here we are!

LULA. Are you sure this is the right place?

BEAUTY. If Father's directions were accurate, it is. He *said* "second castle on the right after you pass the dragon's cave."

LULA. But how can we be sure that was the dragon's cave he *meant?* I mean, you see one dragon's cave, you've seen them all. (*SAM, a bit testily, clears his throat loudly.*) They all tend to look alike — charred rocks around the entrance, smoky haze permeating the air, and that strong sulfur smell . . . (*SAM clears his throat even louder, and manages to elbow LULA gently; she turns, reacts.*) Oh, Sam! I'm so sorry! Yes, you can put the bags down now. (*He does so, gratefully, against*

52

wall below doorway, then—on all fours—will explore room a bit, sniffing at table-legs, etc., during:)

BEAUTY. (*moving further into room, looking up at ceiling, around at furnishings, etc.*) Well, Beast or not, if this is his home, he certainly knows a lot about elegant living!

LULA. It *is* impressive . . . and yet, there's somehow an aura of fear and doom and danger about it.

BEAUTY. Well, what would you *expect* to find in a Beast's castle?! I'm *sure* we've found the right one, aren't *you?*

LULA. (*shivers, hugs herself briefly*) I wish I *weren't!* (*MUSIC INTROS, and she sings:*)
It's like a palace!
Such elegance, such grace,
And sweet sense of malice . . .
This must be the place!

(*SAM, still exploring, will move toward archway as BEAUTY joins song and strolls tableward.*)

BEAUTY.
I'll just be taking
A chair, and sit, in case
My knees won't stop shaking . . .
(*sits in chair*)
This must be the place!

(*There comes a ROAR from offstage* U.L., *and SAM— who has just peeked through archway in that direction—reacts with terror, scurries* D *of bed, lies down on his stomach with his face out front, and puts both paws over his eyes, during:*)

LULA. (*rushes up to BEAUTY*)
There's someone coming!
Oh, please hold my hand!

(*Shadow of BEAST appears centered on corridor wall
as standing LULA and seated BEAUTY hug and
clutch at one another in terror.*)

BEAUTY.
My heart is drumming
Quiet like a bongo band!

(*BEAST springs into view at center of archway.*)

BOTH WOMEN.
He's here! He's fearsome!
Don't look at his face!
(*They release one another so that each can put her
hands over her eyes.*)
If somewhere we've gotta die,
This must be the place!

(*MUSIC softens as BEAST moves gently toward them.*)

BEAST.
You mustn't be distraught.
You're far too overwrought.
While you are here,
Be of good cheer.
Your fears are all for nought.
So, ladies . . .
(*They will cautiously uncover eyes, not yet
unafraid, but no longer as fearful.*)
Don't be tearful.
Your pulses need not race.

BOTH. (*holding one another again*)
     For feeling quite fearful,
     This must be the place!
BEAST. (*moves to bureau, begins holding up items of clothing and jewelry from its drawers, during:*)
     You'll be a smash in
     These jewels, silks and lace!
BOTH. (*moving timidly-but-interestedly toward bureau area*)
     For fright fraught with fashion,
     This must be the place!
BEAUTY. (*taking a gown and holding it in place against herself, admiring it greatly*)
     But hearts could calm in
     A fabulous gown . . .
LULA. (*holding and studying, but not donning, a tiara*)
     Or feel no qualm in
     A ruby-crusted crown . . .
BEAST. (*Places an amicable arm over their shoulders, holding them nearer to him on either side, to which they react with forced, uneasy smiles.*)
     The life I offer,
     You soon will embrace!
     In time you'll find you can trust me!
BOTH.
     In time you may not disgust me!
ALL.
     For fast-changing attitudes, this must be
     Just the place!

(*At song's end, growing very nervous in his proximity, BEAUTY and LULA each take one step down and away to the side from him, facing out front, still with forced, uneasy smiles.*)

BEAST. Ladies, you are far too fearful. I mean you no harm. You have no reason to cower and cringe.

LULA. That's all *you* know!

BEAUTY. After all, castle or not, riches or not, there is always the worry about where we two shall wind up at the dinner hour! (*SAM raises his head, uncovering his eyes.*)

SAM. Wurf.

BEAUTY. Okay. We *three!* (*SAM gives satisfied nod, lowers head, re-covers eyes.*)

BEAST. If that is all that is bothering you, dear lady — by the way, which of you is the one called "Beauty"?

LULA. (*surprised but far from displeased*) You mean you can't *tell?!*

BEAUTY. Now, don't be hard on the poor old Beast — perhaps he simply lacks an eye for loveliness! (*to him, with a curtsey*) *I* am Beauty.

LULA. (*similarly*) And my name is Lula. (*as she straightens:*) But *why* need we not worry about the dinner hour?

BEAST. Because by then — if all goes well — I may be freed of my enchantment and no longer a danger to you or to anyone else. (*At this, SAM uncovers eyes and raises head again.*)

SAM. (*hopefully*) Wurf?

BEAST. Yes, it's quite true, Sam — at least, I *assume* you are Sam?

SAM. (*rises to his knees, nods vigorously*) Wurf!

BEAST. Sam, what would you do if I told you there was a big bowl of beef bones out on the floor of the kitchen? (*For answer, SAM springs to his two feet, does a little jig, pirouette and — if manageable — cartwheel, then ends in a down-on-one-knee-with-arms-outflung "Jolson Finish" out front.*) That's what I thought. Well, the kitchen is second door to your right down the corridor. (*SAM springs up, scurries on all fours to almost exit* L. *at archway, but stops long enough to come back, rub his cheek alongside BEAST's knee, panting happily, then finally completes his exit.*)

LULA. Do you know — I'm feeling better already. A Beast who is kind to animals can't be all that beastly.

BEAUTY. Unless it's only "professional courtsey"? I mean, beasts usually tend to stick together. (*dismisses the notion with a shrug*) Oh, well, there are more important matters to attend to. (*faces BEAST, holds up gown*) Is there someplace I can change into this? I would dearly *love* to get out of my farmer's-daughter dress and into something so much more suitable for a person of my radiant gorgeousness!

BEAST. Well — yes, there is — first door past the kitchen. But — do you not wish to hear how I might be relieved of my bestial curse?

BEAUTY. Oh. Well. I suppose so. But will it take long?

BEAST. I'll be as brief as I possibly can.

LULA. Then, by all means, let us hear about it, Beast. Oh, dear! I shouldn't use that as a *name!* What *does* one call you?

BEAST. "Beast" will do quite nicely, Lula, thank you.

BEAUTY. Will you both please cease all these polite amenities and get on with the bit about the curse?

BEAST. Sorry, Beauty. Sit down, ladies, while I tell you about it. (*BEAUTY will re-seat herself on chair, moving it down alongside* L. *edge of table, and LULA will sit on* U *corner of foot of bed, BEAST more-or-less centered between them, during:*)

LULA. Thank you, Beast.

BEAUTY. Lula, you're interrupting!

LULA. Sorry. Go ahead, Beast.

BEAST. Well, it was like this— (*MUSIC INTROS, and he sings:*)
    I was not always thus as you view me.
    I was once young and handsome and good.
    But my fate became dusky and gloomy
    When I met with a witch in the wood!
LULA.
    Oh, please set your sad story before me,
    For I'm certain your fate was unjust.
BEAUTY.
    I suspect this is going to bore me,
    But do tell us your tale, if you must.

(*BEAST can now move from his position to farther* D, *so that he can move about, gesture, pantomime what he's singing about, etc., and we can see the women full-face—LULA's always sweetly caring, BEAUTY's almost always distracted and less than enthralled—as he continues:*)

BEAST.
    Not too far from this spot
    Where the forest is silent and shady,
    And the star twinkles not,
    I encountered an ugly old lady.
    From the sack on her back
    Came aromas that sent my heart crooning,
    And I said, "Is that bread?",
    For from hunger I fairly was swooning!
BEAUTY.
    That reminds me, I do like a snack before bed.
    Are your servants alseep or have they fallen dead?

LULA.
  Beauty, please have some manners!
  The Beast isn't through.
BEAUTY.
  Oh, all right, Beast, continue!
  But hurry up, do.
BEAST.
  From her bag she withdrew
  Bread and cheese that looked so satisfying,
  And the hag let me chew
  Bread and cheese till my hunger went flying.
  Then I offered a coin
  Before I off on my merry way went.
  But she scoffed, "No, let's join
  Our two mouths in a kiss for repayment!"
BEAUTY.
  Well, a deal is a deal!
  Now, may *I* have some food?
BEAST.
  But I haven't completed
  The tale I would tell.
LULA.
  Let the poor Beast continue;
  We mustn't be rude!
BEAUTY.
  One more minute, then I say
  Ta-ta and farewell!
BEAST. (*a bit annoyed, but he sings a bit faster*)
  Woe is me! For instead
  Of repaying as asked, I just lightly
  And quite gleefully said,
  "I would never kiss one so unsightly!"
  Then her curse rocked my world

And today with that curse I am laden.
Here's the curse that she hurled:
"Be a Beast, then, till kissed by fair maiden!"
Then off on her broom the old lady arose!

BEAUTY. (*rising, stretching*)
Well, that's life! Now, excuse me,
I'm starting to doze!
(*moves toward archway; BEAST, now near doors,
turns u to face her and explain:*)

BEAST.
But you don't understand!
It is *your* kiss I lack!

BEAUTY. (*faces down toward him for:*)
Kiss a Beast? There's a laugh!
Now it's time at last to have my snack!
(*exits L. via corridor, proudly, head high*)

BEAST. (*crushed, slumps, leans mournfully against
wall u of door, staring out into garden*) I was afraid of
this. She cannot abide my horrid aspect. My doom is
sealed.

LULA. (*stands up, rushes to him, takes his hand*)
Please do not despair. She may start feeling differently
as the dinner hour draws near!

BEAST. (*laughs ruefully*) Oh, but I would *never* dine
upon one so lovely as she!

LULA. (*releases his hand, presses her fingertips to her
cheeks, gazing out front for:*) Oh, dear.

BEAST. (*places a hand fondly on her shoulder*) Or
upon one so sweet and kind as you.

LULA. Well, *there's* good news! Oh, but, poor Beast,
how will you *ever* persuade her to break the evil spell
that lies upon you?

BEAST. Perhaps by kindness, by somehow touching
her heart before the three days are up.

LULA. *What* three days?

BEAST. Oh, that was *another* part of the curse: Once the lovely maiden is in my power, I have three days to convince her to kiss me — if I do not succeed — I curl up and die.

LULA. How come you didn't sing that part of the curse in your song?

BEAST. (*shrugs*) I couldn't think of a rhyme for "deadline."

LULA. (*laughs*) Then you should have asked for help! What about "headline" — or "bread line"?

BEAST. Lula, there's no way to put *today's news* or the *depression* into a lilting lyric!

LULA. You've got a point.

BEAST. Now, if you'll excuse me, I'm going out into the garden and brood. (*exits* R.)

LULA. That poor creature! Doomed to remain hideous — yes, even doomed to *die* — unless he receives that kiss! But will Beauty *do* it? Will the kiss work if she *does* do it? Or will the Beast just pine away and die? Will the end of the third day see doom and destruction or a typical happy ending? How in the *world* will this story turn *out?* (*points a finger out at audience*) Stay tuned!

(*Then, as she turns and heads* U, *MAXINE does her thing, the card flips to "THE FARM," then MAXINE exits, and LIGHTS COME UP on the farm setting; after a moment, FATHER and HOLGA enter* L., *heads bowed, shoulders slumped, feet dragging, overnight bags in hand; they get near* UC, *then stop wearily, and set bags down.*)

FATHER. Home. Home at last. I never thought I'd be this glad to see the old homestead!

HOLGA. It's even nice to *smell* it!

FATHER. As the old saying goes — "The nicest thing about a vacation is that it doesn't last forever!"

HOLGA. (*nods*) Heaven be praised. (*MUSIC INTROS, and:*)

FATHER. (*sings*)
Any time you go sojourning,
You get smarter while you roam —

HOLGA.
For, the lesson that you learn is
That you should've stayed at home!

BOTH.
Such a time we had!
Though it should have been a honey,
We were running out of money in a week!
Such a time we had!
With nobody to befriend you,
Sailing down the Seine could send you
Up the creek!

HOLGA.
When your French is quite poor,
And you fancy that you're
Buying chicken, they bring out a pickled eel!

FATHER.
When you try to complain,
They will register disdain
And then stick you in a room in the Bastille!

Such a time we had!
First we found our reservations
Gave hotel accommodations in a slum!

HOLGA.
And if that's not bad,
Then we tipped a man to guide us
To a table right beside the kettledrum!

FATHER.
    And you learn, your first night
    In the City of Light,
    Even gendarmes don't go walking after dark!
HOLGA.
    And if wine you will sip
    Till you have to take a trip,
    You'll find bathrooms in the middle of a park!
BOTH.
    Such a time we had!
    With the palms we had to grease there,
    It's no wonder the Parisian survives!
    Though we're rather glad
    That we had our little caper,
    We're much gladder to escape here with our lives!

(*At song's end, HOLGA picks up the bags, while FATHER moves to chair and sits.*)

FATHER. I think I'll rest here in the sun for awhile. All that Parisian nightlife has me feeling kinda pale.

HOLGA. That's right, darling, you rest up. I'll just go unpack the bags and start doing some laundry. (*Then BOTH look up as SAM, an envelope in his mouth, comes running in from* D.R.; *he stops beside FATHER.*)

HOLGA. Oh, look, it's Sam!

SAM. (*moving his head to indicate envelope*) Wurf!

FATHER. And he seems to have a message! (*takes envelope, opens it*) Do you suppose it could be a letter from the girls?

HOLGA. Either that, or the Beast needs some after-dinner mints. (*will set down bags and move to FATHER, during:*)

FATHER. Ah! It's a note from Beauty! (*starts reading*)

HOLGA. Can't you read it out loud? I haven't got my glasses on.

FATHER. What? Oh, sure. Lemme see, now — oh, yeah. Well, she says: "Dearest Father . . . and Reasonably Dear Holga . . ."

HOLGA. Hasn't changed a bit, has she!

FATHER. Do you want me to read this, or don't you?

HOLGA. Sorry. Go on.

FATHER. Uh — oh, yeah. "It is dreadful here. I hate it. All these beautiful clothes, and lovely jewelry, and marvelous food — "

HOLGA. *I* should have such suffering!

FATHER. Shush! ". . . and marvelous food, and lovely castle, are such a bore, with no handsome prince to share it with. You *must* get me out of here! I don't care how. Make up some urgent reason I am needed home at once."

HOLGA. Like what, the lounge chair misses her rear end?

FATHER. Holga — !

HOLGA. Okay-okay, go on.

FATHER. "I can't stand it another minute. I hate it, I hate it, I hate it. Signed, Beauty. P.S.: Make it snappy."

HOLGA. Oh, well. I suppose we really should try to help her . . . though I'll be darned if I know what use she'll be back here!

FATHER. Let's see. What kind of urgent message can we send? (*will take pad and pencil from pocket, poise pencil point over pad, during:*) Earthquake, flood, tornado?

HOLGA. Of course not. *Those* are reasons to stay *away* from home! Better tell her you're dying.

FATHER. But that would be a lie.

HOLGA. Not entirely. All the way home from Paris,

you've been telling me you're *half-dead* from the trip, so *that* much is true.

FATHER. Oh . . . okay, I guess you're right. (*starts scribbling note, during:*)

HOLGA. I wonder how Lula is making out? Not that I expect Beauty to even *notice* another *woman's* mood. I sure hope *she* didn't wind up on the dinner menu!

FATHER. (*now folding note and putting it into envelope*) Beauty said the food was delicious. She'd *never* say that about her *stepsister!*

HOLGA. Well, that's true enough.

FATHER. Here, Sam, take the note back to Beauty. (*FATHER puts envelope in SAM's mouth.*)

HOLGA. Do you think she'll bring *Lula* with her when she returns?

FATHER. Well, if I'm supposed to be dying, would Lula stay *away?*

HOLGA. Of course not, but what if Beauty doesn't read her the note?

FATHER. Lula's bound to ask questions when she sees Beauty packing to go.

HOLGA. But what if she doesn't *see* her packing?

(*NOTE: From the moment he got the envelope back, SAM's business has been this: He starts for D.R. immediately, but stops and comes back to chair on HOLGA's line — then starts off again on FATHER's next line — back on HOLGA's next line, etc.; now, after final speech, above, SAM stands up on two feet, folds his arms in exasperation, and pointedly taps one foot to show his impatience.*)

FATHER. It'll be *fine*, Holga, just *fine!* (*turns to*

SAM) So scram, Sam! (*SAM drops to all fours, exits* D.R.)

HOLGA. Now there's nothing to do but wait.

FATHER. (*stands up from chair*) That's all *you* know! Dying man or not — I'm hungry!

HOLGA. (*will retrieve bags as they head* U) I'm not sure if there's any food in the house . . . oh, wait! I *did* bring along some fancy food from our trip!

FATHER. Great! I could eat a horse!

HOLGA. It's french-fried squid.

FATHER. I'd prefer the horse.

(*And, as they exit* U, *MAXINE does her thing, the sign is flipped to "THE CASTLE," and as she exits and LIGHTS COME UP FULL, we find BEAUTY in bed, the BEAST [head* U] *on the cot at the foot of her bed, and LULA [head* L.] *in the sleeping bag at the foot of the cot. [See stage diagram]*)

BEAUTY. (*sits up*) Oh, it's morning again!

BEAST. (*sits up*) The morning of the third day!

LULA. (*sits up*) Oh, dear! Time passes so fast when you're having fun!

BEAUTY. Sleeping with a Beast at my feet isn't *my* idea of fun!

(*TRIO will get variously out of bed, cot and sleeping bag over ensuing dialogue; BEAST is dressed as before, but WOMEN are in lovely nightgowns.*)

BEAST. I couldn't take a chance on you waking up with the urge to kiss me, and not be close by.

BEAUTY. Believe me, you had nothing to worry about.

LULA. But it *might* have worked — after all, some people *walk* in their sleep — maybe you might be the kind who *kisses* in her sleep. (*LULA will roll up bag and replace it on dresser, and BEAST will fold up cot and replace it in corner, over dialogue, now; BEAUTY, of course, ignores the rumpled bedding she just left and heads* U.)

BEAUTY. Excuse me, I've got to get dressed. (*yawning and stretching, exits* L. *via corridor*)

BEAST. (*as they work on bag and cot*) Do you know, Lula — for a beautiful girl, Beauty is kind of a pain.

LULA. It took you two full days to find that out?

BEAST. I was kind of blinded to her temperament by her loveliness — especially since, according to that old witch, the maiden who kisses away the spell must be the most breathtakingly beautiful maiden in the world. And Beauty certainly is that.

LULA. It's a shame she's so stingy with her kisses. Tell you what — (*has bag rolled, now, and heads for dresser, while BEAST, with cot folded, heads for corner*) you could tie her down, I'd stand behind her with my hands on her cheeks to force her lips into a pucker, and —

BEAST. (*laughs ruefully*) How I wish that would do the trick! But no; the witch was most specific about it. The maiden must bestow her kiss willingly, or it doesn't count.

LULA. That makes sense. Wouldn't be much of a curse if all you had to do to break the spell was run out and *force* a kiss from a girl!

BEAST. Well, maybe I'll be lucky. Maybe there *is* someone more lovely than she, and these three days won't count against me. I mean, I'm *assuming* she's the most beautiful — she's certainly the most beautiful *I've* ever seen — ah, but if a more beautiful girl does exist — !

LULA. You still have a chance to live! (*rushes to him,*

takes his hands) Oh, Beast, Beast! Wouldn't that be miraculous!

BEAST. It certainly would. And — do you know — I'd almost *rather* it were some girl other than Beauty. She'd never believe it, but — between you and me — *I'm* just as repelled at the thought of *her* kiss as *she* is at the thought of *mine!*

LULA. Oh, I *do* hope you're right. Because — well — there's something about you that makes me feel so — so — oh, never mind.

BEAST. No. Please. Tell me, Lula.

LULA. Well, it's just that — even with that dreadful face of yours — I rather *like* you, Beast.

BEAST. And I rather like *you,* Lula. It would be so marvelous if *you* were the one who could shatter this spell. If *you* could be the certain someone to restore me to myself! (*MUSIC INTROS, and he sings:*)

How my heart is searching for someone,
That special someone who'll share her love,
With a kiss to sweetly disarm that
Enchanted charm that I'm pris'ner of!
Despair would vanish in her embrace!
Her kiss could banish this fearsome face!
I'm ever hungering for someone to sunder
This spell I'm under, that holds me fast!
When will I see that someone
Of beauty unsurpassed . . .
That someone who will save me at last?

LULA. (*Her arms go about him, and she rests her head against his chest [facing down front, of course], as she sings:*)

I am also searching for someone,
A certain someone with love to vow.
Someone who will care for me only,

Someone as lonely as I am now!
My dreams have told me there must appear
Someone who'll hold me forever near!
(*Leans away from him enough so that they can look into each other's face as they finish:*)
BOTH.
Could it be that you are that someone,
That certain someone,
That dream-come-true?
With you I feel a feeling
Like nothing hitherto . . .
Perhaps I'm seeking someone like you!

(*At song's end, the irresistible happens; they zero in, slowly, for a kiss—but just before they connect, BEAUTY [now elegantly gowned] appears in archway.*)

BEAUTY. Well! (*They spring apart, guiltily.*) I might have known! Lula, dearest, I knew you were hard up for a lover, but *really!*

BEAST. Now, Beauty—

BEAUTY. And you! All that fine talk about how you needed my kiss so very desperately! And the moment I turn my pretty back, you are dallying with the likes of Lula! Well, if you think I'd kiss you now, you're crazy!

BEAST. But—we only—oh, what's the use! I'll go see about breakfast! (*BEAST exits u.*)

BEAUTY. Well, Lula? I am awaiting an explanation of your conduct!

LULA. (*moves toward dresser*) And I will gladly give you all the explanation you deserve. (*Takes lovely gown from dresser, proceeds to dress, humming echo of her duet with BEAST half to herself; it takes BEAUTY a few seconds to realize what this end-of-conversation means; then:*)

BEAUTY. Oh! How unutterably rude! (*sits petulantly in chair*) All *I* can say is, I pity you. I always *have* pitied you. It must be dreadful, knowing you'll go through life totally plain and completely unattractive to men, and probably die a bitter old spinster!

LULA. (*has moved* D *a bit, and is busy fixing her furbelows or lacing her blouse or fussing with her farthingales, or whatever, somehow no longer to be irritated or browbeaten by BEAUTY*) That's all *you* know! (*MUSIC INTROS, and while she completes her costume, she sings:*)

Someday someone will suddenly
Come around and say he's found
True love with me!
Someday someone just truly might
Tell me he wants me to be
His heart's delight!
He'll bow to me and softly take
My hand and tell me that I make
His heart start to sing
Like anything!
Yes, someday someone both strong and shy
Will recognize and realize
There's more to me than meets the eye!
Then he'll hold me
And kiss my troubles away . . .
When someone comes from somewhere,
Someday!

(*Now the melodic shoe is on the other foot, and as LULA repeats her song, BEAUTY—seated angrily in that chair* U *of her—adds her own lyrics.*)

BEAUTY.
> That girl! That girl!
> That unattractive churl!
> Someone should tell her that,
> With all due respect,
> No man would select
> That girl! That girl!
> She'd make his stomach twirl!
> He'd be too sick to choose her!
> No man woos a total loser!
> Unalluring, barely pretty —
> Well, perhaps she'd provoke his pity!
> That girl! That girl!
> No prince or even earl
> Would stoop to give her greeting,
> Let along set up a meeting
> 'Neath the stars
> While strumming sweet guitars!
> Oh, no, I really must concur
> No man would like the likes of her!
> Love she'll never stir
> In a connoisseur!
> No man could prefer
> That girl!

(*At song's end, BEAST appears in archway; his costume now includes chef's cap and apron.*)

BEAST. Come and get it, ladies.
BEAUTY. (*stands*) It certainly took you long enough! I am simply famished! (*Then, before they can exit, SAM comes bounding in at door, envelope in mouth.*)
SAM. Wurf!

LULA. Why, Sam, what have you got there? (*takes envelope*) Beauty, this is addressed to you!

BEAUTY. Then *give* it to me! (*snatches envelope, rips it open, grabs out note, reads it, then tosses note and envelope onto table, and pat-a-cakes her hands in glee*) Oh, Lula! Beast! The most marvelous news! (*and even before they can ask what, she announces:*) Father is *dying!*

BEAST. What?!

LULA. How terrible!

BEAUTY. (*moving doorward*) So of course, I *must* go to the poor man at *once!* Sorry to be so hasty, but he's *such* an old poop he probably won't last *long!*

BEAST. But this is the final day of my enchantment — if you don't release me with your kiss —

BEAUTY. Now, *really,* Beast! I have to go see a *dying man!*

BEAST. Could you not even kiss me goodbye?

LULA. Yes, Beauty! I mean — if you *don't* kiss him, it *will* be goodbye!

BEAUTY. I'm sorry, but I must smile my prettiest at Father's bedside, and I could hardly do that after kissing a Beast! (*exits, SAM scurrying after her*)

LULA. Oh, dear! Father dying! *I* should go, too — but — how can I leave you — not knowing how you are, or if the spell —

BEAST. (*places a fingertip on her lips*) Hush, Lula. You must go, of course. I understand. Besides, you're my only ally — perhaps you may be able to persuade Beauty to return before the time is too late.

LULA. But how will I know? I mean, if she *is* the one, you are doomed, should she not return. But if she is not, I would certainly want to know that you were still alive!

BEAST. All right, then. Here . . . (*moves to bureau,*

takes small handmirror from drawer) This is a magic mirror. When you wish to see me, look into its depths, and you shall. (*returns, hands it to her, doffs chef's cap*) Take it with you. And — as you must surely know — it is not *all* that belongs to me that you take with you!

LULA. (*takes mirror, stifles a sob, starts to exit, then turns for:*) Beast . . . I love you.

BEAST. Yes. I've know that for some time, now. And *I* —

LULA. Yes?

BEAST. (*with more confidence than he feels*) Well — time enough to talk about that when you return.

LULA. (*miserable*) Yes. Time enough. Time enough. (*starts to sob, so turns and exits, fast*)

BEAST. (*to himself*) Goodbye. Goodbye . . . my love . . .

(*Sighs, looks at chef's cap in his hand, abruptly hurls it onto floor and stalks off; MAXINE does her thing, card flips to "THE FARM," and when LIGHTS COME UP FULL, farmyard is empty except for SAM, who is asleep on lounge — on his back, with that reflector held loosely under his furry chin; a moment later, BEAUTY and LULA hurry on D.R, see SAM, and stop.*)

BEAUTY. So *that's* why he was in such a hurry to get here first! Sam! (*He jumps up.*) Get out of my chair at once! How *can* you think of sunning yourself when I've had such a narrow escape! (*HOLGA enters UC.*)

HOLGA. Aha! You made it! Welcome back, kids! How's things?!

LULA. More important, how is *Father?*

HOLGA. Him? Oh, he's sleeping.

LULA. That's good. A rest might be the very thing he needs.

HOLGA. (*guiltily*) Say, Lula — about that message — I don't want you upset about it —

LULA. Mother — what are you trying to tell me?

HOLGA. Well, you see — (*loses her nerve*) Listen, maybe your Father should tell you, himself. I'll just go see if he's awake . . .

LULA. But you mustn't *disturb* him in *his* condition — !

HOLGA. (*backing uneasily toward* UC) Uh . . . right. I'll just — um — peek in on him, and if he's awake, I'll give you girls a call, okay? (*exits* UC *without awaiting an answer*)

LULA. Now, Beauty, when we see him, we mustn't say anything that would lower his spirits. We must appear happy and cheerful, and perhaps it will be contagious!

BEAUTY. But what is there to be so happy and cheerful *about?*

LULA. Oh . . . why . . . well, for one thing — we're *home!*

BEAUTY. Yes, that's true. But face it, Lula — we're home on the *farm!*

LULA. Well — we must *still* be cheerful!

BEAUTY. About being on the *farm? How?!*

LULA. Let's just consider all the *positive* points about it!

BEAUTY. *That* shouldn't take very long! (*shrugs, moves down beside LULA*) But *I'm* game if *you* are! (*MUSIC INTROS, and:*)

BOTH. (*will dance, hoedown-style, as they sing:*)
We're back where we're mixin' swill
So early that the rooster's still in bed!
We're back where our biggest thrill
Is seein' that the pigs are all well-fed!

Delight discontinues
(*BOTH flex biceps.*)
As you grow bulging sinews on your arm . . .
Back on the farm!

LULA.

It's great to be among the cows and horses
On our Daddy's little spread.

BEAUTY.

The only problem that occurs, of course, is
That we're wishin' we were dead!

BOTH.

A farm is just a lot of dust
Surrounded by manure!

LULA.

But we act glad —

BEAUTY.

For dear old Dad —

BOTH.

To our discomfiture!
When we're back where the cornfield quakes as
Weevils and the cutworms have their brunch!
We're back spendin' coffeebreaks by
Slaughterin' a chicken for our lunch!
It really is hell to
Know we must say farewell to girlish charm . . .
Back on the farm!

BEAUTY.

To milk the cow is a catastrophe so
Damp and chillin' to the bone!

LULA.

With fingers colder than an icecube, we know
We're not sufferin' alone!

BEAUTY.

That cow would love the comfort of
A flannel pantaloon!

LULA.
'Cause milkin's how we got that cow
To jump over the moon!
BOTH.
We gave up a castle to re-
Turn where all the chores are drab, and just
Too ghastly to wrassel with! We
Oughta let the Beast recapture us!
We'd run to him madly,
And we would very gladly —
BEAUTY.
Let him crack us on a rack —
LULA.
Or keep us tied up in a sack —
BOTH.
If it meant we could turn our back . . .
On the farm!

(*At song's end, BOTH are laughing and slapping one another on the back; FATHER and HOLGA will enter, unnoticed, during:*)

LULA. Beauty, I didn't know you had it in you! I've never *seen* you expend so much all-out energy before!

BEAUTY. (*very uneasy*) Well — Father was never *dying,* before!

LULA. Father! Oh, dear! How could I have forgotten! Imagine, you and I out here in the yard singing up a storm, while all the time our dear Father is — (*starts to turn houseward, reacts*) Right *behind* us?!

HOLGA. Lula, your father is — uh — feeling much, much better!

LULA. (*very suspicious now*) Father — what *is* this?! (*FATHER, HOLGA and BEAUTY look at one another, guiltily, unable to speak for a moment; then:*)

FATHER. (*inspired, drops to his knees, arms outflung sideways, face heavenward, for:*) It's a *mir-a-cle!*

HOLGA. (*doing the same*) *Hal*-la-loo!

BEAUTY. (*ditto*) Praise be! (*SAM — a natural-born critic — gives an unbelieving howl at their attempt, lowers his chin to the ground, and covers his eyes with his paws.*)

LULA. Okay, all of you! Up off your knees! Let's have a little leveling around here! (*TRIO will get to their feet, during:*)

BEAUTY. *I* never said Father was ill —!

HOLGA. But she *asked* him to —!

FATHER. In a note she sent with *Sam!* (*LULA looks accusingly at SAM, who — still prone — props himself up on his elbows, and does a fingers-outward, palms-upward shrug of embarrassment.*)

LULA. You stinkers! All of you! Playing silly games, while that poor suffering Beast might be, any minute now, curling up and —

(*ALL fall silent and bewildered as we hear a shrill and repeated "BEEP! . . . bee-BEEP! . . . bee-BEEP! . . ." as on a physician's away-from-the-office pocket beeper.*)

BEAUTY. What in the world —?!

LULA. (*first to realize*) The Magic Mirror! (*grabs it out of her purse, pocket, or where she's kept it, stops the beeper, hesitates, then hands it to BEAUTY, averting her eyes*) Here! *You* do it! I can't look!

BEAUTY. All right! (*peers deep into mirror, deeper and deeper; than her eyes widen, her jaw drops, and she screams:*) Oh no! This is horrible! Ghastly! Totally tragic!

OTHERS. *What?!*

BEAUTY. (*turns her head their way, one forefinger pressing a spot in the center of her cheek*) I'm getting a *zit!*

LULA. (*gives a growl of exasperation, grabs mirror back*) Oh, *gimme* that, *I'll* look! (*does so; her face grows fearful*) Oh, no! This *is* terrible! He's just — *lying* there! . . . *Oh!*

OTHERS. *Now* what?!

LULA. The mirror's gone *blank!* (*drops mirror on chair, starts* D.R.) I've got to *go* to him!

FATHER. Lula, you can't! It's nearly nightfall!

HOLGA. She's got to, you stupid lummox, can't you see that? Come on, let's go *with* her!

BEAUTY. (*As they start after LULA, who is just exiting.*) Listen, while you're gone, what should *I* do. . . ?

FATHER. *You* can tend the *farm!*

BEAUTY. (*glances back at farmhouse, shudders*) That's all *you* know! (*just as FATHER and HOLGA exit:*) Wait! I'm coming with you!

(*She exits after them; SAM, alone, stands on two feet, turns his head their way, then out front, then finds a coin somewhere, flips it, catches it, looks at it, shrugs, and exits after BEAUTY; then MAXINE does her thing [NOTE: To sustain the mood of the next scene, BEAST must not assist in the set-change, but be already on the bed when it pivots into view], flips the card to "THE CASTLE," exits, LIGHTS COME UP, and we find BEAST on his back on the bed, eyes closed, hands folded on his chest; he is under the coverlet, which is partly folded downward, from his folded hands on down; a moment after the lights come up, LULA rushes in, then FATHER, HOLGA, BEAUTY and SAM rush in behind her [NOTE: SAM will remain on two feet for the remainder of the show]; LULA has stopped, just near the foot of the bed, shocked; the OTHERS stop just short of her; then, silently, they go one-by-one to stand along the upper edge of bed, looking down upon BEAST, BEAUTY nearest the pillow.)*

LULA. He's . . . not moving . . . not breathing . . .

FATHER. I guess it's . . . too late . . .

HOLGA. Nothing we can do for the poor creature, now . . .

LULA. *Yes!* Yes, there *is* something! The sun hasn't set just yet! The day isn't officially over! Beauty — *you* can save him! *Only* you!

BEAUTY. You don't mean — *kiss* him?! *Uccch!*

LULA. It's the only way to break the spell — to save his life! Please, Beauty, please!

BEAUTY. I — I can't! I just can't! I don't want to see the creature die, but — I'm sorry — nothing in the *world* could make me kiss him!

HOLGA. (*clutches FATHER's arm*) *Do* something! Make her kiss him! She'll obey you! After all, she's your daughter!

FATHER. (*reacts with surprise*) *My* daughter?! *I* always thought she was *your* daughter!

HOLGA. But she came to the house with you when we were married!

FATHER. Hell, I thought she was one of the bridesmaids!

BOTH. Just who *are* you, *anyhow!*

BEAUTY. (*shrugs*) I was passing the church on your wedding day. I knew I was too beautiful to ever go to work for a living. And I knew how very befuddled newlyweds can be. So I tagged along.

FATHER. Of all the nerve!

HOLGA. Of all the gall!

FATHER. Eating us outa house and home—

HOLGA. And sunbathing while we worked!

LULA. Listen, I don't care *whose* daughter she is! She's the only one can save my precious Beast, and the sun will set in ten minutes! Beauty—if you won't do it for us—do it for the newspapers!

BEAUTY. (*brightens*) Newspapers? What newspapers?

LULA. He is a rich and powerful man. If you save his life, you'll be a heroine. Your picture will be on every front page in the country! And that *prince* of yours may see it!

BEAUTY. Oh! Of course! Why didn't you *say* so! (*instantly bends and gives BEAST a glorious kiss*) There! I did it!

HOLGA. But he's still lying there . . .

FATHER. And he's still not breathing . . .

LULA. Oh, no! No! We were too late, after all!

BEAUTY. (*realizes the significance of this*) Ucch! (*wipes mouth with back of hand in disgust*)

LULA. (*drops to her knees at foot of bed, her face against BEAST's feet under the coverlet*) My darling! My dearest darling! Oh, my heart is just breaking! What will I do? Whatever will I do without you? (*buries face against bed, sobs piteously*)

FATHER. (*Hurries to help her to her feet; OTHERS also moves into a sympathetic circle around her.*) Now-now, darling. You did your best. Come along home, now.

LULA. I can't. I can't. It's wrong to just leave him lying there!

FATHER. Hush, now, baby . . . we'll cover him up, then we can go.

(*Still holding LULA, makes urgent head-gesture to the OTHERS to do something; HOLGA, BEAUTY and SAM immediately move along* downside *of bed, and pull the coverlet up over the BEAST's face [NOTE: It is* very *important that they be on the* downside, *blocking the audience's view of BEAST in a shoulder-to-shoulder formation, because in this moment, BEAST-player must* remove *wigged mask and gloves and drop them out of sight over* U *edge of bed, before the coverlet is placed to hide him from head to foot.]; this being done, they move to FATHER, who starts moving the still-sobbing LULA toward door.*)

LULA. No! Wait! Let's at least — sing a hymn or something!

HOLGA. Honey, the sun will be gone in *five* minutes, now! We don't have the time!

BEAUTY. We'll be lucky if we make it home at *all!*

LULA. One song of farewell! Is that too much to ask?

FATHER. No. Of course it isn't. Come on, everybody! (*GROUP moves to* U *edge of bed, now, with LULA nearest pillow; SAM, one paw over his heart, is nearest foot of bed; he won't sing along with others, but will match their every gesture.*)

BEAUTY. I'm not sure if I *know* any hymns . . .

FATHER. (*so sternly that she cringes*) Then we'll *make* one up! (*then MUSIC INTROS, and:*)

ALL. (*gesture at figure on bed*)
There he lies! The beast is dead!
(*OTHERS gesture at BEAUTY, who doesn't sing next phrase.*)
Her kisses came too late to end

His dreadful metamorphosis!
(*ALL shakes heads, and BEAUTY rejoins singers, on:*)
No more we'll detest him!
(*palm-to-palm in prayer, looking heavenward*)
May Heaven rest him!
(*do right-face and shuffle slowly doorward*)
Well, we've done our mournful duty.
(*pause and gesture back toward corpse*)
There he lies because of Beauty!
GROUP/BEAUTY.
If she'd/I'd shared her/my kiss
In time he'd be released . . .
But, like we said,
He's quite deceased.
The poor old Beast is dead!

(*At song's end, ALL shuffle in slow-motion chug-chug unison, heads bowed down, toward door; LULA, last in the line, is almost out door, when:*)

LULA. No! I can't! Can't leave him! (*rushes back to u of bedside, while OTHERS re-enter just a step, remaining in door area*) Not without — saying goodbye — the way he would have wanted it! (*And with that, she lifts the near-edge of coverlet, just enough so that she, and not we, can see his face, bends down, and tenderly [unseen] kisses him; she holds kiss a moment, then abruptly stands up away from him, her face shocked and surprised.*) Oh! He — he — he kissed me back! (*Then she realizes.*) He's alive!

(*Then the coverlet is flung down and away from BEAST [and we will no longer call him that], and we see that it is BEAU, young and handsome as ever.*)

ALL OTHERS. *Beau!*

BEAU. (*springs up from bed, clasps LULA in his arms*) Yes, it is I! I went off to seek my fortune — met that old witch in the woods — and the rest you know!

BEAUTY. But I don't understand! The spell could be broken only by a kiss from the loveliest girl in the world — and I kissed you — and nothing happened!

BEAU. That is because *you* are only beautiful on the *outside,* Beauty. But Lula is beautiful where it counts — in the deepest depths of her loving heart!

LULA. Oh, Beau!

BEAU. Oh, Lula! (*They kiss.*)

FATHER. Oh, Holga, isn't love wonderful!

HOLGA. Let's try it and see! (*They kiss.*)

BEAUTY. It's not fair! It's not! This castle — the beautiful clothes — the jewels — the food — the wine — ! All will go to plain little Lula, instead of beautiful, deserving me!

BEAU. Oh, no, Beauty. There you are wrong. This castle is not mine. I am still only a lowly farmer. But even so, I hope that Lula will not hold it against me, and marry me regardless!

LULA. Oh, Beau — you *know* I will!

BEAUTY. I don't understand — if this castle and all that goes with it doesn't belong to *you* — whom *does* it belong to?

BEAU. Why, to a handsome young millionaire, who was *also* under a witch's spell, and who now — thanks to the power of Lula's loving heart — has been freed from *his* enchantment, too!

OTHERS. Then where *is* he?

SAM. Right here! (*and he lifts off the dog-head, and we see that it is HARRY — cigar and all*)

BEAUTY. (*rushes to him at once*) You are a millionaire?

HARRY. A *multi*-millionaire!

BEAUTY. And the spell is broken?

HARRY. For now and forever!

BEAUTY. Would you — uh — like to have a wife?

HARRY. I'd like nothing better!

BEAUTY. Oh, marvelous! Then say those three little words that will make your dream of marital bliss come true!

HARRY. All right. I will! (*takes a deep breath, then calls loudly:*) Hit it, Baby!

(*And MAXINE tippy-taps onstage, now garbed in a mini-skirted wedding outfit, with spangled white tap shoes; her MUSIC this time is somewhat briefer [see musical score], but it's enough to get her into HARRY's area — where, with her right hand on his shoulder, she does the same pose-finish she used to do at the easel.*)

LULA. Oh, isn't this wonderful! I have Beau, Father has Mother, and Sam has this sweet little escapee from the Rockettes!

HARRY. The name is Harry — and this here is my beloved Maxine! (*to MAXINE*) Didn't I *tell* you you'd wind up with a millionaire, Baby?!

MAXINE. But Harry — the millionare part is only a role in a show — you're not *really* a millionaire!

HARRY. What's the difference? *You're* not really a tap-dancer! (*looks toward LULA*) "Rockettes"? You gotta be kidding!

BEAUTY. It's not fair! Everybody's got somebody, and I'm left all alone!

HARRY. Relax! As a millionaire, I can give you the one thing your heart has always desired!

OTHERS. *And what is that?*

HARRY. (*with an isn't-it-obvious? shrug*) Her very own full-length mirror!

BEAUTY. (*a shriek of total rapture*) *Wheeeee!* Isn't this simply marvelous?!

BEAU/LULA. It's even better than *that!* (*MUSIC INTROS and they sing:*)

> Isn't it kinda great?
> Isn't it supersonic?
> Doesn't our love make
> Casanova's seem platonic?
> Isn't it kinda swell?
> Doesn't it ring that bell,
> Giving our lips a demonstration
> Of a nifty new sensation?
> Isn't it kinda right
> Outa the melodramas?
> Doesn't it make us feel like
> We're the cat's pajamas?
> Isn't it kinda strong?
> Pardon me if I'm wrong,
> But wasn't it kinda Love to come along?

(*MUSIC CONTINUES, and—pay attention—here is the pattern that will prevail in this finale: They have moved down front of OTHERS for their song-segment; now, as next part of song starts, they dance backward* U, *and next singers dance* D *toward us on "interlude melody" which follows, timing interlude so that they are in* D, *position when they lilt into the "Isn't it . . . etc." part of song; thus:*)

FATHER/HOLGA. (*dancing down*)
We agree
It's great to see

Those two in fond embrace!
But our love's
More certain of
A certain change of pace! Oh . . .

Isn't it kinda great?
Isn't it quick and easy?
Doesn't it beat those nights
We'd meet to play Parcheesi?
Whatta we need with plows?
Whatta we need with cows?
Holding you close, dear, where's the harm
In striving to forget the farm?
Oh, isn't it kinda fun
Making our dentures rattle?
Isn't a kiss a lot more bliss
Than raising cattle?
Holding off pitching hay
Really can make our day,
So wasn't it kinda Love to come our way?

HARRY/MAXINE. (*dancing down as FATHER/ HOLGA dance up*)
Sakes above,
Their kinda love's
Like falling off a log.
But love's keener
When between a
Dancer and a dog! Oh . . .

Isn't it kinda great?
Isn't it roly-poly?
Isn't it wine, "Sweet Adeline"
And mostaciolli?
Isn't it sirloin steak?

Wouldn't it frost the cake?
Isn't it everlasting glory,
Not to mention hunky-dory?
Isn't it where it's at?
Isn't it sunny weather,
Knowing what hums or goes all thumbs
We'll be together?
Doesn't it give a glow
Lighting us head-to-toe?
And wasn't it kinda Love to say hello?
(*Now they dance-switch with BEAUTY during:*)
BEAUTY.
   As for me,
Why should love be
Between a gal and guy?
To my mind,
Where could I find
A love so true as I? So . . .

Isn't it kinda great?
Could it be any dearer?
What could be less than to possess
A full-length mirror?
Isn't it just a pip
Taking an ego-trip?
Wouldn't you love the chance to dig your
Own sweet face and fancy figure?
Shouldn't I faithfully
Make it my daily duty
Just to inspect my own electric
Brand of beauty?
Won't my own image be
All that I want to see?
And wasn't it kinda Love to favor me?

(*This time, OTHERS come down during interlude to flank BEAUTY for the Big Finish, during:*)

ALL.
   When we shout
   And sing about
   The one each one adores,
   Trying to sum
   Up Love becomes
   A string of metaphors, like . . .
   Isn't it kinda great?
   Isn't it dry martini?
WOMEN.
   Isn't it pie?
MEN.
   And ham-on-rye?
ALL.
   And fried zucchini?
MEN.
   Isn't it Polish ham?
WOMEN.
   Isn't it curried lamb?
ALL. (*hands briefly to stomachs, for:*)
   Isn't a romance great and grand which
   Makes you wish you had a sandwich?
WOMEN.
   Isn't it egg foo yung?
MEN.
   Isn't it pickled herring?
ALL. (*as tempo slows to more romantic rhythms*)
   Isn't it something really
   Far beyond comparing?
   Isn't it shining bright?
   Doesn't it hit the height?
   (*the Big Finish, out front*)
   And wasn't it kinda Love to turn out right?

(*LIGHTS FADE SLOWLY TO BLACK as ALL sustain
final chord and MUSIC MOVES TO ITS FINISH;
then comes the curtain-call—to lavishly wild applause—and the LIGHTS DIM FOR THE LAST
TIME.*)

END OF SHOW

Alternating Setting
for
"BEAUTY AND THE BEAST. REALLY."

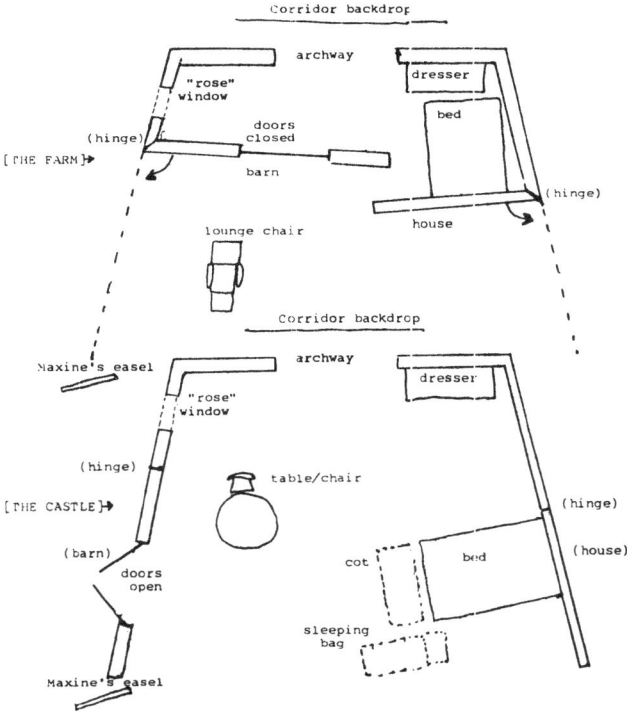

Also By

Rick Abbot

DRACULA: THE MUSICAL?

PLAY ON!

BUT WHY BUMP OFF BARNABY?

A TURN FOR THE NURSE

JUNE GROOM

SKIN DEEP
Jon Lonoff

Comedy / 2m, 2f / Interior Unit Set

In *Skin Deep*, a large, lovable, lonely-heart, named Maureen Mulligan, gives romance one last shot on a blind-date with sweet awkward Joseph Spinelli; she's learned to pepper her speech with jokes to hide insecurities about her weight and appearance, while he's almost dangerously forthright, saying everything that comes to his mind. They both know they're perfect for each other, and in time they come to admit it.

They were set up on the date by Maureen's sister Sheila and her husband Squire, who are having problems of their own: Sheila undergoes a non-stop series of cosmetic surgeries to hang onto the attractive and much-desired Squire, who may or may not have long ago held designs on Maureen, who introduced him to Sheila. With Maureen particularly vulnerable to both hurting and being hurt, the time is ripe for all these unspoken issues to bubble to the surface.

"Warm-hearted comedy … the laughter was literally show-stopping. A winning play, with enough good-humored laughs and sentiment to keep you smiling from beginning to end."
– *TalkinBroadway.com*

"It's a little Paddy Chayefsky, a lot Neil Simon and a quick-witted, intelligent voyage into the not-so-tranquil seas of middle-aged love and dating. The dialogue is crackling and hilarious; the plot simple but well-turned; the characters endearing and quirky; and lurking beneath the merriment is so much heartache that you'll stand up and cheer when the unlikely couple makes it to the inevitable final clinch."
– *NYTheatreWorld.Com*

COCKEYED
William Missouri Downs

Comedy / 3m, 1f / Unit Set

Phil, an average nice guy, is madly in love with the beautiful Sophia. The only problem is that she's unaware of his existence. He tries to introduce himself but she looks right through him. When Phil discovers Sophia has a glass eye, he thinks that might be the problem, but soon realizes that she really can't see him. Perhaps he is caught in a philosophical hyperspace or dualistic reality or perhaps beautiful women are just unaware of nice guys. Armed only with a B.A. in philosophy, Phil sets out to prove his existence and win Sophia's heart. This fast moving farce is the winner of the HotCity Theatre's GreenHouse New Play Festival. The St. Louis Post-Dispatch called Cockeyed a clever romantic comedy, Talkin' Broadway called it "hilarious," while Playback Magazine said that it was "fresh and invigorating."

Winner!
of the HotCity Theatre GreenHouse New Play Festival

"Rocking with laughter...hilarious...polished and engaging work draws heavily on the age-old conventions of farce: improbable situations, exaggerated characters, amazing coincidences, absurd misunderstandings, people hiding in closets and barely missing each other as they run in and out of doors...full of comic momentum as Cockeyed hurtles toward its conclusion."
–Talkin' Broadway

THE OFFICE PLAYS
Two full length plays by Adam Bock

THE RECEPTIONIST
Comedy / 2m, 2f / Interior
At the start of a typical day in the Northeast Office, Beverly deals effortlessly with ringing phones and her colleague's romantic troubles. But the appearance of a charming rep from the Central Office disrupts the friendly routine. And as the true nature of the company's business becomes apparent, The Receptionist raises disquieting, provocative questions about the consequences of complicity with evil.

"...Mr. Bock's poisoned Post-it note of a play."
– New York Times

"Bock's intense initial focus on the routine goes to the heart of *The Receptionist's* pointed, painfully timely allegory... elliptical, provocative play..."
– Time Out New York

THE THUGS
Comedy / 2m, 6f / Interior
The Obie Award winning dark comedy about work, thunder and the mysterious things that are happening on the 9th floor of a big law firm. When a group of temps try to discover the secrets that lurk in the hidden crevices of their workplace, they realize they would rather believe in gossip and rumors than face dangerous realities.

"Bock starts you off giggling, but leaves you with a chill."
– Time Out New York

"... a delightfully paranoid little nightmare that is both more chillingly realistic and pointedly absurd than anything John Grisham ever dreamed up."
– New York Times

BLUE YONDER
Kate Aspengren

Dramatic Comedy / Monolgues and scenes
12f (can be performed with as few as 4 with doubling) / Unit Set

A familiar adage states, "Men may work from sun to sun, but women's work is never done." In Blue Yonder, the audience meets twelve mesmerizing and eccentric women including a flight instructor, a firefighter, a stuntwoman, a woman who donates body parts, an employment counselor, a professional softball player, a surgical nurse professional baseball player, and a daredevil who plays with dynamite among others. Through the monologues, each woman examines her life's work and explores the career that she has found. Or that has found her.

www.ingramcontent.com/pod-product-compliance
Lightning Source LLC
Chambersburg PA
CBHW070241140726
47909CB00018B/1440